W9-BMY-896

She hoped tonight she might have some time with Victor alone. Tonight she would tell him how she felt, if he didn't tell her.

A knock sounded at the door.

She carefully made her way across to the door and pulled it open.

Her mouth dropped in stunned shock.

Victor stood there, dressed in what had to be a very expensive tux, waiting to be allowed in.

"I take it you like it?" he asked, mildly amused.

"I—wow!" She blushed. He was every bit the movie star now.

He walked in and turned to her, taking her hands. "You are a fresh breath of beauty in a world too old and cynical, my dear."

"I feel like Cinderella at the ball," she said lightly.

Lucy Dundore

Books by Cheryl Wolverton

Love Inspired

*Hill Creek, Texas
†Everyday Heroes

CHERYL WOLVERTON

RITA® Award finalist Cheryl Wolverton has well over a dozen books to her name. Her very popular *Hill Creek, Texas,* series has been a finalist in many contests. Having grown up in Oklahoma, lived in Kentucky, Texas, Louisiana and now home once more in Oklahoma, Cheryl and her husband of more than twenty years and their two children, Jeremiah and Christina, always considered themselves Oklahomans transplanted to grow and flourish in the South. Readers are always welcome to contact her at P.O. Box 106, Faxon, OK 73540, or e-mail at Cheryl@cherylwolverton.com. You can also visit her Web site at www.cherylwolverton.com.

AMONG THE TULIPS

CHERYL WOLVERTON

Love Inspired

Published by Steeple Hill Books™

If you purchased this book without a cover you should be aware
that this book is stolen property. It was reported as "unsold and
destroyed" to the publisher, and neither the author nor the
publisher has received any payment for this "stripped book."

STEEPLE HILL BOOKS

Steeple
Hill®

ISBN 0-373-87267-4

AMONG THE TULIPS

Copyright © 2004 by Cheryl Wolverton

All rights reserved. Except for use in any review, the reproduction
or utilization of this work in whole or in part in any form by any
electronic, mechanical or other means, now known or hereafter
invented, including xerography, photocopying and recording, or in
any information storage or retrieval system, is forbidden without
the written permission of the editorial office, Steeple Hill Books,
233 Broadway, New York, NY 10279 U.S.A.

All characters in this book have no existence outside the imagination of
the author and have no relation whatsoever to anyone bearing the same
name or names. They are not even distantly inspired by any individual
known or unknown to the author, and all incidents are pure invention.

This edition published by arrangement with Steeple Hill Books.

® and TM are trademarks of Steeple Hill Books, used under license.
Trademarks indicated with ® are registered in the United States Patent
and Trademark Office, the Canadian Trade Marks Office and in other
countries.

www.SteepleHill.com

Printed in U.S.A.

You say, "I am rich; I have acquired wealth and do not need a thing." But you do not realize that you are wretched, pitiful, poor, blind and naked. I counsel you to buy from me gold refined in the fire, so you can become rich.

—*Revelations* 3:17-18.

My family, for helping clean and do laundry
while this story poured out of me!
Thanks Steve, Christina and Jeremiah.

And my online friends,
who are always so supportive and helpful.

Prologue

You say, 'I am rich; I have acquired wealth and do not need a thing.' But you do not realize that you are wretched, pitiful, poor, blind and naked. I counsel you to buy from me gold refined in the fire, so you can become rich...
Revelation 3: 17, 18

"It's going to be your fortieth birthday. That calls for something really special. I say go for it!"

Thirty-nine-year-old Annie Hooper glanced at blond Cynthia, one of the friends she was having her early birthday dinner with. She shook her mousy brown-haired head at her fairer friend and thought again how different the two looked. Cynthia looked fresh from a salon while Annie felt she looked like…a mother. "I don't even know where I'd go. Besides, the kids need me." Annie laid down her fork and lifted her napkin to pat her lips.

"Susan and Mark?" Amy piped up, her auburn eyebrows shooting up with a bit of disbelief. "Oh, come on, Annie. Mark is thirty-three and has a great job and Susan is thirty-two and is working as a nurse. Face it. Your stepkids are grown and need to stop depending on you for everything. They certainly don't need you here providing food and shelter for them. You have to start living again. You're still young."

Although Susan and Mark weren't officially her children, she thought of them as such, though they rarely called her Mom. No, they had their real mother, with whom they still stayed in contact. After running a hand through her hair she sighed. Unfortunately, the kids always had a way of guilting her into staying at home when she tried to plan something, like last year when she'd said she had been going to get a passport and had actually brought home some travel brochures. But her friends were right. She was young; the kids were older, so shouldn't she start living again?

Annie dropped her napkin on the table.

Her two friends sighed in unison.

They knew that wasn't all that was bothering

her. "The kids still miss their dad," Annie said simply. She leaned back in the cushioned chair covered in lovely mauve brocade.

"It's been four years," Cynthia replied. "They need to move on with their life. *You* need to move on with your life." She too had finished her lunch. She nodded as the waitress took her empty plate.

It had been four years since Annie had lost her husband. They had been hard years in some ways, lonely years as well. Sometimes his death seemed as if it happened only yesterday, especially when problems were building up or the kids were pulling a number on her. At night, however, when she was alone in bed or watching something on TV, it seemed as if he'd been gone forever.

"You always said when Harry retired, you were going to go somewhere different for a real vacation," Amy added. "I know you got your passport last year with just such an intention." Amy took the last bite of her dessert and then handed her plate to the waitress.

Yes, Annie had gotten her passport. In a fit of frustration and desperation she'd decided she was going on a trip. Her kids, however, had been aghast that she'd forgotten their daddy so easily and was going to traipse off into the unknown.

"Your kids like knowing you're there so they

can bum more of Daddy's money off you—" Cynthia started.

"And get you to do their laundry—" Amy added.

"This isn't about their dad being gone," Cynthia finished.

Annie lifted her water glass and took a sip, allowing the ice-cold water to wash down her throat and take away the building tension.

"I just don't know if I can travel there by myself or even if I should." Frustration slipped in, and she silently prayed for guidance. "It's crazy. I've always had someone there making the decisions for me and now…"

"And now you're allowing your children to do that for you," Cynthia said gently.

"Honey, you deserve to get away." Amy picked up her iced tea and took a leisurely sip of the light golden brew. "You should go for it."

"I don't think I could simply up and leave the family. What would the kids do?"

How would the children react if she decided to go on this trip? Though Annie knew they used her and it was wearying, she still felt a responsibility for them.

That's what it boiled down to. When she'd married Harry, she'd inherited a young boy and his younger sister as immediate family. She'd been thrown into instant adulthood trying to raise two children.

Looking back, she realized she hadn't been ready for it. She'd been a child herself really at 17. She'd done her best, but had her best been good enough? The children's mother had never forgiven Harry for marrying Annie. And on every weekend and holiday that Michaela had had the children, she'd done her best to poison them against her.

Annie also had church responsibilities as well as friends there. Although most of her friends were gone, uncomfortable being around a widow or simply no longer having anything in common, she had one or two who she saw occasionally, including Amy and Cynthia. However, she was going to be starting a new job this fall as an art teacher at a local community center, and so this would make the perfect time to go—if she so chose.

"The kids depend too much on you," Cynthia informed her. "They use you and you allow it."

That hurt. Cynthia was always the blunter of her two friends. And she never spared what she thought.

"You deserve this time," Amy added more diplomatically. "You'll never get to splurge again like this. You know that. Once you settle down into this new job, you'll be too caught up in life to consider doing something so wild."

Doing something wild. Was that what she was doing?

Annie shook her head. "I'm not sure I'm the wild sort—"

"Well maybe you should be," Cynthia cut in. "It's time you had a chance to live a little. You married Harry while you were still in high school, for Pete's sake. It's time for you to go out and have fun."

Annie thought about what her friend said. She was going to be forty next week.

Forty.

And she'd never left Louisiana.

"Where would you like to go?" Amy prodded.

Annie smiled slightly. "Holland."

She could talk about her dreams at least. What would that hurt?

"Holland? What is in Holland?" Cynthia demanded.

Annie shrugged. "Tulips."

All three women burst into laughter. Annie honestly didn't know what Holland had to offer. She simply thought it would be fun to visit somewhere she'd never been, somewhere off the beaten path.

"Think of the tours you could take," Amy added, when the laughter died down.

"We'd even help you pack," Cynthia chimed in.

"Whoa, wait a minute. I'm only dreaming here. Let's not get carried away." Annie shook her head, trying to slow the two women down.

"Why not get carried away?" Cynthia asked.

Annie tried to think of a reason but couldn't come up with a legitimate one.

Cynthia leaned forward and took her hand. "This is your chance. Get away for the summer. Spend time doing some soul searching. We'll take care of the house and your cat. We'll make sure everything runs smoothly while you're gone. Just take this time for yourself, Annie. You need it."

Annie couldn't believe she was wavering in this. Wasn't this the time of her life when things were supposed to slow down? She should be spending her time at home, enjoying the quiet solitude.

Of course, she'd been doing that for four years now. Four years. Where had that time gone? What had become of her during that time? Herself as a person? Had she ever been her own person? An individual with her own feelings and thoughts?

Had she ever had a life? she wondered now. One of her own? Or was she always going to be defined by her marriage and family?

If she were honest, Harry had rarely been there. She had wondered at one time if he was having an affair, but had then decided it was simply that he was a workaholic.

Annie had no idea who she was anymore. She'd come to that realization as she'd sat at home one day, wondering when her stepdaughter was going to drop by.

Maybe a vacation was exactly what she needed. Time away from all the memories and time to find herself. Time to spend with God.

"The kids will have a fit."

Amy shrugged. "They'll handle it."

"They'll have to," Cynthia added and then, seeing the hesitation on Annie's face, added, "If they need you, you can always give them your number. Besides, their mom lives in town."

Annie knew the kids would be worried without her there. She met with her daughter at least once a week and her son usually stopped by on weekends with his laundry and had lunch with her. He still didn't do his own laundry.

A month or so without laundry. Now that would be odd.

"I can tell you're considering it," Amy said with glee in her voice. "Come on. Cynthia, can you take an extra hour or so before going home? I say we go look at brochures at the travel agency. We'll have her on that plane by next week."

"That soon!" Annie said, worry in her voice.

Amy laughed with enthusiasm. "Sure. Why not? The sooner the better."

"I agree. I know you, Annie. If we don't rush you out the door and onto the plane, then you'll end up staying put."

Annie sighed. "You're right about that."

"We have a surprise for you." Cynthia reached into her purse, which was set next to her feet on the elegant carpeted floor.

Annie lifted her napkin and folded it neatly before releasing it. "You've already bought me lunch. What else are you planning?"

These two women really were her dear friends, but they knew how to keep her off balance.

Amy grinned. "It's our gift. We had to make sure first that you'd use it."

Annie glanced from one to the other, her cheeks warming. "I'm too old to get gifts. Just going out to lunch was enough."

"Oh, no, honey," Cynthia said and then presented her with a small gold oblong box. "We wanted to make sure about our plans before we gave this to you. Open it."

Annie smiled and obediently opened the checkbook-size box. When she pulled out the piece of paper her jaw dropped open. "This is a gift certificate from a travel agency."

Amy chuckled. "It's enough for a ticket just about anywhere in the world, and if you choose

Holland, then it will even cover most of the hotel cost.''

''Oh, dear.'' Annie stared in shock at what she held.

Cynthia smiled. ''You can choose anywhere.'' She hesitated and then added, ''If you don't use it, you can roll it over until next summer.''

''Yeah,'' Amy added and accepted the receipt from the waiter. She quickly scanned the price and pulled out some money, tossing it on the table with the check. She then stood. ''Come on. Let's go to the travel agency and we'll see what we can find.''

''I'm not certain I'm going yet.'' Annie gripped the unbelievable gift in her hands, staring at it, still in shock.

Talking about it was one thing—but actually leaving Louisiana and the kids?

Cynthia grinned. ''That's okay. We'll just look.''

Annie knew that against the two of them she had no defenses. She didn't with her kids either. That was one of her big problems; she enjoyed going along with life and, unfortunately, that could have bad as well as good results.

In this case she wasn't sure which it would be.

But the idea of a month away…

How bad could it be?

Especially since they were only looking.

Chapter One

Haut, Holland: One week later

Tires screeched. Metal boomed against metal. All forward motion in the car stopped, except for Annie who suddenly flew forward, still propelled by Newton's Law. Her hands lost their grip on the steering wheel. Pain erupted in her legs, her chest, her head as she met the resistance of the abrupt cessation of the vehicle.

Stars danced in brilliant colors before her eyes.

A wreck.

She'd been in a wreck.

Vaguely she heard noises around her, but as for focusing, that wasn't possible.

Drums pounded in her ears as she sat trying not to pass out.

Her first day in Holland.

Her entire body throbbed in pain. Forcing her eyes open, she groaned as the bright light from the sunny day increased the throbbing agony in her head. Absently she reached for her head but stopped as she saw people coming toward the car—including an angry looking man who was stalking his way to her, looking for all the world as though he was going to tear her apart as soon as he got close enough.

Short, round and wearing an apron, he shook his meaty fist before pounding on her window. With each slap to her window, her head pounded out a cadence of objection to the noise.

He shouted, loudly, in Dutch.

Her head nearly exploded.

She had to calm him down, had to apologize, make him understand that she hadn't meant to hit his car. What was she doing? Why had she come here? Did they arrest foreigners for auto accidents?

Lifting her hand to her aching head, she felt something wet and sticky. Glancing at her fingers, she saw her hand come away with blood. *Oh dear.* She felt dizzy and turned her head away from the sight.

She couldn't help her eyes from slipping closed.

Her hands went to her eyes and pressed gently as if to relieve the headache. "Do you speak English?" she asked.

Alarmed at how weak her voice sounded she tried to speak up. "Does anyone speak English?" When no one answered, she lowered her hands and opened her eyes.

Her window was still up. No one could hear her—and the man still screamed.

Fumbling, she reached for the knob to the window and proceeded to roll it down. "Does anyone speak English?" she repeated, her voice still sounding weak. She hurt from head to toe and didn't think she could move.

The man ignored her question and jerked the car door open.

She gasped as she realized she could move—but it caused her a lot of pain. The throbbing noise in her head increased, drowning out some of her attacker's unintelligible words. He pointed at his car and then back at her.

Had she been in the wrong lane? She tried to remember, but everything was fuzzy. All she could remember was she had been driving down the street on the way to the hotel just outside of town…

She turned to get out of the car. A crowd was gathering. Panic edged up her spine. She had to do something, say something, find someone who could help her. Her chest tightened and her palms grew slick with sweat.

Why hadn't she listened to her son and daughter? They'd both nearly disowned her when she'd told them of her plans last week. She'd seriously considered not coming, but Cynthia and Amy had convinced her she would have a great time.

She reached up and grasped her head. It pounded viciously from her movements. The front window of the car was smashed. She must have contacted it with her head. That would explain the lump that was forming on her forehead as well as the blood.

Pushing herself around, she gasped in pain as she moved her right leg. Looking down she saw both knees were bloody too.

Hearing the murmurs, she glanced carefully back up.

"Does *anyone* speak English?" A large crowd swarmed around, talking and pointing. A mob? Did they have mobs here? What would they do to her? Her vision narrowed as she felt herself breathing faster.

Oh no. She had never been in a situation like this. Never. She tried to slow her breathing.

A policeman appeared and started asking questions. She wanted to cry.

She couldn't understand a word he said.

Again she asked herself why she had come to Holland.

"English. Eng-lish!" she cried out.

"Do you need some help?" The deep baritone voice came from in the crowd. Desperately she looked around, trying to find who had spoken.

The crowd obviously knew. People turned, pointed and started babbling.

The noise level doubled, which in turn, doubled her headache. "Please, yes. Who said that?"

She reached for the car door, intending to stand.

"I did."

A tall man, at least six foot, stepped forward as the crowd parted. Dressed in a pair of casual jeans and paint-splattered top, he looked vaguely familiar—American, she thought. Long hair to his shoulders, slightly wavy and pulled back in a ponytail, and deep blue-gray eyes; he had a casualness that bespoke comfort in his surroundings.

Funny she should notice all of that about a stranger. "I can't understand the policeman. I'm a tourist."

The man turned and spoke to the officer, who in turn motioned for the people to move back. Another officer showed up and began directing people out of the way.

The man who had been yelling at her now turned to the officer and began telling him something in rapid-fire Holland-ese. What language did they speak? She didn't remember.

Finally her link to the local language turned back to her. "Are you hurt?"

Insurance papers. Driver's license. What all was she supposed to show the officer? "Yes."

Annie gripped the side of the car and the door and started to lift herself out.

"Wait—" the American said.

The first bit of weight on Annie's right leg told her more than anything else that she really wasn't okay.

She cried out in pain and pitched forward—right into the arms of the American.

She saw stars, and then, the next thing she knew, she was lying in the man's lap on the sidewalk, staring up at a blue sky.

"Why did I do this?" she moaned.

"I tried to warn you that sometimes shock will prevent a person from noticing injuries. Now lie still until we can get you to a hospital."

Annie blinked. Warm strong arms surrounded her, holding her gently.

"Who are you?" she asked, more than willing to take his advice because moving, she decided, wasn't a priority.

"Call me Victor," he said simply.

She nodded, or tried to. She realized Victor was

holding a hankie to the lump on her head. "Ow." The pressure hurt.

He gentled his ministrations. "You have a small cut there."

"I want to go home," Annie whispered.

She could hear all of the voices around her, and she had never been so frightened in her life. She trembled from the pit of her stomach to the limbs of her body. She lifted her hand and saw her fingers shake with a palsy of shock and pain.

"I just turned forty, you see. My friends thought this vacation would be a wonderful idea. I didn't think about the language problem or driving or…anything. We just made reservations for today, my birthday and then I got on the pl-pl-plane. Well, yesterday in America, you see. I was on my way to the hotel when th-th-this accident happened. I only want to go ho-ho-home now."

She realized she was rambling, and worse, she realized tears had filled her eyes and had spilled over. *Oh heavens. Dear God, please help me get control,* she silently prayed.

Victor reached up and brushed away the tears before pulling her closer. "It's shock and an adrenaline rush. Don't worry. It's going to be all right. Let's take one thing at a time. First, let's get you taken care of, okay?"

In the distance, a siren's blare grew louder—a

very odd foreign-sounding siren that made her feel so much more alone and different. Annie bit her lip. "But the hospitals overseas…I've heard stories…and I don't speak the language…"

"Let me handle this," the man said gently.

She nodded. "I'm so-so-sorry."

"For what?" he asked.

The siren died down as an ambulance pulled up.

"For getting you involved, for taking this trip— I don't know—for many things."

Two men got out and approached her.

As they knelt next to her, Victor asked, "Is your husband here with you? Someone I need to notify?"

Annie shook her head slightly, immediately regretting it. "No. I'm a widow."

Victor released her, gently laying her down on the sidewalk and then stepped back to allow the men to get to her. She didn't move. She hurt too much to move.

"I don't suppose I can have your name," he said.

Annie realized she hadn't told him. "Annie. Annie Hooper."

"Nice to meet you, Annie," the polite stranger said.

"You have no idea how nice it is to meet you," Annie said, meaning it with every heartbeat.

She was terrified and alone. She was exhausted after the long trip and all she had been thinking about was getting to the hotel to rest.

She had no idea what had happened. She had been driving and now she was being loaded onto a gurney. How had the wreck occurred? A big blank was there where information should be. And where was the man she'd hit?

As the two men lifted her, she couldn't help a surge of panic. "Don't leave me," she called and realized the man who had been at her side was once again talking to the police. He immediately turned and stepped over to her. Wrapping both of his hands around hers in an intimate act of great comfort, he focused his complete attention on her, his eyes connecting and holding hers in a steadying gaze. "I'm right here."

She bit her lip, embarrassed, but unwilling to let go. "Thank you."

Some trip this was turning out to be. Yet, holding on to this man calmed her somewhat. A needle pricked her arm as the paramedics started on IV and then injected a clear fluid into the IV line. "What are they giving me?"

Her rescuer turned and rattled off a question in that language they spoke.

The one attendant answered.

Tall dark and handsome turned back to her. "Something to help calm you."

Oh heavens…she could already feel it taking affect. "You look funny," she said, but it didn't sound right. The words had come out mixed up.

The man smiled, two dimples appearing in his slightly bearded cheeks. "I have a funny look?"

"No. You…your face…it's…turning…" She lifted one hand to show him how he seemed suddenly tilted, but found the effort too much and dropped her hand back to her side. "I'm not making sense."

The attendants lifted the gurney. It felt very odd—as if she were suddenly floating up into the air. Victor was still next to her, however.

"You have a dimple in your chin," she said, staring at him.

He gave her a half grin as he turned to say something to someone near them.

"I would have seen it better if you had shaved. You have stubble all over your face."

He glanced back, his eyes widening in surprise.

She felt the silliest urge to giggle—which she did. And then she closed her eyes.

Until she was jarred.

"Wait a minute. We're moving." She glanced around and noted they were in the back of a vehicle and it was speeding down the street.

Victor was still there, sitting right next to her, along with a stranger who was talking on a radio. Victor held her hand with both of his. He must have sensed her confusion, however, because he released her hand with his right hand and cupped her cheek. ''The medicine is affecting you. We're on the way to the hospital. Obviously time isn't the same for you. We've already been in here several minutes. They must have given you something pretty strong.''

Annie felt disconnected, though his hand felt great. With a sigh she rubbed her cheek against his hand. ''You feel so good,'' she murmured sleepily. ''I had no idea how much I missed a gentle touch.'' She hadn't said that out loud—had she? Ah well, what did it matter? He was here now, with her. Her eyelids felt heavy. ''My protector.''

She didn't want to let her eyes close though and forced them open. The gorgeous guy in front of her was her only lifeline to this world she was in. She didn't want to lose him.

He had an odd look on his face.

She studied him, wondering just who this man was, this gentle soul who had been willing to help her.

''What are you thinking?'' he asked.

''Please don't leave me alone.'' That sounded so wimpish and frightened. She wasn't wimpish

and easily frightened. At least, she didn't think so.
"Yes, I am. Very wimpish."

The man laughed.

She felt his hand against her cheek again and
smiled. "Thank you," she whispered. Turning her
cheek into his hand she snuggled down into it,
thinking it felt so much like her mom's hand had
so many years ago—soft, gentle and caring. She
closed her eyes.

"Thank you again? For what?" Victor asked.
When she didn't answer, he realized Annie was
asleep. Turning to the attendant he spoke in Dutch,
"I want to make sure we get her into a room immediately."

The young tech nodded, a bit starry-eyed. "Of
course, Mr. Rivers. Whatever you want."

Victor simply nodded. He was used to the def-
erence he received, though it did get old. In this
case, however, it would be beneficial; it would en-
sure that 'Annie' got good medical care.

What was he going to do with the woman?

A stranger in a strange land and she didn't speak
the language.

He would love to have a talk with her friends.
Didn't people realize just how dangerous it was to
be in a foreign country where she couldn't speak
the language? If she'd been in one of the bigger
cities, she wouldn't have had a problem, but in the

tiny city of Haut, with a population of only ten thousand, located out in the middle of nowhere—very few spoke English.

Wearily, he shook his head. He couldn't help but worry about Annie Hooper.

And things did happen to innocent people—look at her and the wreck.

Victor always tried to be prepared and ready for whatever might come. It was a good thing in his life—to make sure he was prepared. Not being prepared could lead to national embarrassments.

He hadn't been prepared for Annie, however.

He was surprised that she didn't speak a single word of Dutch or German.

She had rattled him, that was for sure. He'd actually been surprised by her sweet innocent smile. He'd smiled when she'd rubbed up against his hand. Her skin was soft and smooth and smelled of something sweet. He'd never smelled that scent before but it drifted up from her as she'd moved her head. Perhaps a shampoo or perfume. And then she'd commented on his chin. Some women were put off by the dimple, but she seemed to like it, though he wasn't sure about her feelings regarding the light bit of beard he'd worn for his last movie. His long hair and beard were leftovers, and he hadn't cut them yet.

Of course, the drugs were affecting Annie. She'd been slurring every word she spoke.

If he had his way, he would prefer her to be in a different hospital. But since he was there, he would make sure she was treated right.

He frowned. "She is going to be okay?" he asked the attendant.

The attendant shrugged. "She probably has a fractured tibia or fibula and possibly a concussion. Normally we wouldn't give meds so strong, but she's a tourist and pretty unsettled. Americans," the technician said disrespectfully and then winced. "Except for you, Mr. Rivers. Your mother was from Holland so you're not really American, exactly."

Victor thought that attitude was typical and sighed. "It's not important."

As if to make up for his lapse, the attendant sat up straighter and examined the patient more closely. "She could have internal injuries. The doctor will let you know."

They pulled into the entrance to the hospital.

The technician leaned forward and wiped away the blood that was running along Annie's hairline.

Victor didn't care too much for real blood.

Then he realized his own hands had her blood on them, in quite another sense.

He hoped she wasn't seriously injured.

She was actually very pretty in a simple sort of way—innocent, perhaps. She didn't have that world-weary look that so many of his friends did.

In the circles he traveled, it was rare to see someone that looked so fresh at…forty, she'd said?

Forty.

He would have guessed her much younger.

She was only two years younger than he. He had turned forty-two two months ago.

Annie shifted her head. Victor blanched.

A cross.

She wore a tiny cross around her neck.

All good feelings toward this woman were shoved aside as memories of his parents flooded his mind.

She was a Christian—like them.

How could she be? he wondered. But then she hadn't been herself either.

The bitterness and anger—hidden but always near to his heart—threatened to surface. It would have too if he'd had more time to dwell on it, but just then, the ambulance pulled to a stop at the emergency room entrance. Victor realized he still held Annie's hand.

Releasing it, he stepped back and allowed the technicians to do their job.

He followed the stretcher into the hospital and into the ward. Maybe she just wore the necklace because she liked the look. Besides, not all people who wore crosses were like his parents. His parents hadn't believed in wearing any jewelry, so maybe she wasn't like them at all. Anyway, it didn't matter. She was here alone and needed help. And he would help this woman, regardless of her religious beliefs. He forced those bitter memories away by becoming the persona he had created so many years ago through so many parts.

When the nurse came in, he gave all of the information he could and then stepped away to make a call to his home. He needed some fresh clothes. He also needed to talk to this woman when she woke up.

Of course once she was in her right mind and had calmed down, she would recognize him and that might pose a problem. But then, he was used to that.

He would simply be prepared for whatever her reaction would be.

He supposed that the sweet innocence he'd perceived would disappear and he would find out just what type of person Annie really was. Money had that effect on people—money and fame. And he had both. Wearily he sighed and accepted that that was how it would be.

Thinking about that, he decided it might not hurt to put in a call to his lawyer as well.

It was going to be a long day.

Chapter Two

Annie groaned.

She heard someone speaking to her, though she couldn't understand him, and then she felt herself being prodded to sit up.

Painfully she opened one eye. And immediately realized she had been unconscious—again.

"A cast?" She looked down at her right leg in dismay. "I'm in a cast."

"You're awake."

Her gaze went past the other beds in the room she was in, and, to her relief, she saw her rescuer coming down the main aisle, the very man who had just spoken. Wow. She hadn't imagined it. He was hot.

His footsteps echoed on the tiled floor. She

could hear other noises from other beds around her, though the curtains blocked her view of the people in the cubicles. Light shone through the windows near where Victor had entered, and she was relieved to realize that not much time must have passed if it was still light out.

"What happened?"

The man who had been prodding her to sit up now pointed at a wheelchair before pointing at the bed.

She didn't understand him.

Victor said something to him, and the man replied. Victor commented again in a sharper tone and the man strode off, not looking back.

"I'm sorry he woke you. I stepped out to freshen up. I thought you'd be okay for a few minutes. I guess I was wrong."

She pointed at the obvious. "I have a broken leg."

Victor nodded. He stopped next to her bed and lifted his hand to touch her just above her eye. "How do you feel?"

She winced in pain, yet at the same time felt her heart flutter at how close this man was. He was really good-looking and somehow, strangely familiar. His magnetism was unbelievable as well. She really liked the change he'd made while she was unconscious. Instead of the paint-spattered shirt and jeans, he wore a casual pair of dress slacks and a tucked-in polo shirt along with a light tan leather jacket.

She forced a breath in and then said, "I really can't thank you enough for all you've done."

He shook his head. "We need to talk."

He waited and stared at her.

She wasn't sure what he wanted.

Disconcerted, he tilted his head. "Do you have any questions for me?" he finally asked as if he knew something she didn't.

She thought a moment and then slowly nodded. Dropping her eyes, she asked, "Do they arrest foreigners for what happened today? I mean I hit some man with my car—where is he, by the way?"

"That's your question?" He sounded surprised.

She lifted her gaze to meet his and found something akin to amazement, or maybe it was perturbed shock, on his face. "I want to go home," she added, thinking perhaps that was what he was wanting to hear.

He let out a breath and simply glanced past her for a moment as if centering his thoughts.

"You're too banged up to travel. The doctor is willing to release you only if someone watches you for the next forty-eight hours."

"But I didn't come here with anyone."

"I know that. I've been on the phone making arrangements. I have a large house. You can stay with me—"

"I don't even know you." Annie leaned back, slightly stunned that he would suggest such a thing.

Okay, now why had that shocked him so much? His mouth fell open. He started to say something and then paused, getting that same strange look on his face that he had had a few minutes ago. Finally he gazed back at her. "I'm the one you were in the wreck with."

"But the man—the one who was yelling? You're the one who helped me."

Confused, she shook her head. Something wasn't adding up.

"He was angry that a tourist was blocking his business. He was easily paid off with a large order for meat." Victor grinned slightly before the serious look returned. "No, Annie. I was coming into town to buy some paints, and a dog ran out in front of me. I cut right in front of you and caused the head-on."

She gaped as her mind tried to process what had really happened. She still couldn't remember a thing other than driving down the street and then opening her eyes and finding herself injured. "Are you okay?" she asked weakly. She had leaned so heavily on this gentleman throughout her ordeal that she hadn't even noticed whether he'd been hurt.

"I have a much better car than yours. My air bag deployed. I'm a little stiff. But to answer your question, I'm fine. It's you who was injured."

"I am so sorry," Annie said, horrified. "You've been so nice. I've relied on you and now—"

"Now I'm inviting you to my house," he said, interrupting her. "Since it was my fault, not yours, there's no reason to keep apologizing and every reason for me to make it up to you by giving you a place to stay while you're here recovering."

He reached out and took her hand, lifting it and wrapping both of his hands around it again. Then he allowed his eyes to drift upward, over the planes of her face until they finally locked with her own brown eyes, and he said simply, "You'll need someone who can interpret for you over the next few days while we get all of this sorted out."

Annie nodded. "But I don't know you."

He shook his head slightly, started to say something and then let it go.

"The doctor does. Everyone in this small town does," he said. "If you need references, ask the doctor if I'm safe."

At that moment an older man came walking up with a chart in his hands.

Victor dropped Annie's hand and turned toward

the doctor. They proceeded to have a rapid-fire conversation in Dutch.

"Like the doctor would understand me if I asked him," Annie muttered.

Evidently she'd muttered it too loudly because both men turned toward her. "Ask me what?" the older man said in heavily accented English.

"You speak—"

"—English? Yes. There are few of us in town who do." He smiled. "I'm Dr. Gaulkner."

"She wants to know if it's safe to stay with me until she recovers," Victor interjected into the conversation before Annie could say anything.

The doctor lifted his eyebrows and turned toward Victor. He laughed outright. "Safe? Now what a question. Many people, they would appreciate to answer that."

Turning back to Annie he said, "He is more safe than staying in an hotel alone. And if that no reassures you, I'll give you mine home phone number where that you can contact me. You should be grateful that Victor, he is taking such time out of his schedule to tend for you."

He smiled at Victor. "If you have the questions about mine instructions I've given you for her, you ring me." He scribbled something on a piece of paper and handed it to Annie.

It was a set of numbers.

"Mine number. Ring me up."

He turned and walked away.

"Wait. How much do I owe? Where do I pay? Do you take travelers' checks?" She gasped, her hand going to her mouth. "Oh, no, they're in the car!" Panic built again.

"It's already taken care of," Victor said. Catching her hand, he pulled her attention back to him. "I had my driver, who wasn't driving me at the time, by the way, go by and collect your things. Leaving them in an unattended vehicle wouldn't be wise."

He continued to hold her hand, stroking it gently.

She noticed that.

And he had a way of using his eyes that captured and held her attention.

He was a very physical person.

Nervously, she licked her lips.

He smiled slightly, noticing the gesture.

"I'm indebted to you," she said simply.

"Consider it payback for the wreck I caused," he corrected with an odd look on his face.

Finally, she nodded.

"You know, you're not what I expected," he murmured softly.

"Oh?" she asked.

He glanced down at her neck.

She fingered the small cross, not understanding.

He obviously wasn't going to explain. He changed the subject. "Can you stand and move into the wheelchair?"

"Where are my clothes?" she asked, a bit of a blush working its way to her cheeks at having to ask a stranger such a question.

He pointed and she nearly groaned when she realized they were next to her on the end of the bed.

"Let me change," she said, embarrassed that a stranger was standing here, helping her and she was dressed in next to nothing.

He nodded and stepped past the partition, pulling it closed to give her some privacy.

She took stock of her body. She already had some darkening areas on her chest. And her neck and shoulders hurt too. As a matter of fact, her lower back hurt, she realized as she dropped her skirt over her head and buttoned it around her waist. But the pain was pretty blunted. The medication, which muted the pain, made her woozy as well.

"Ready?" Victor called finally.

"Ready," she replied, and thought she was more than ready to sit down as she dropped onto the edge of the bed.

He returned and ran his gaze over her.

"Amazingly enough, it only hurts when I move," she quipped.

"You're still doped up from all the medication they gave you."

She glanced down at her hand and found a small bandage where an IV had once been. "Oh, yuck. I'm a mess." Her clothes were bloody and on her legs, now bare of hose, she could still see some remnants of blood.

"You can have a hot bath when we get home. Come on, let me help you."

He reached up and slipped his hands under her arms.

She gasped at the strength in those hands.

How long had it been since a man had touched her so intimately? The closest she'd been to a man in four years was an occasional hug at church.

It was very disconcerting.

"What is it?"

She glanced up and realized her face was only inches from his. She couldn't help but think how handsome he was and how very masculine.

"Are you hurting?" he prompted when she didn't answer.

Jarred by the second sentence, she nodded. "Everywhere."

He turned with her and helped her into the wheelchair. "I have a housekeeper who'll help you bathe if you need to. In the meantime, let's just concentrate on getting you home and rested. I have a feeling you're going to be hurting a lot more before this is over.''

"I have a feeling you're right." She smiled gently.

The man who had originally woken her up returned with a pair of crutches. He took control of the wheelchair and passed the crutches to Victor. With a smooth motion he turned and wheeled her out of the room. The hall was long, a dingy gray-blue and very old looking. Light bulbs dotted the ceiling along the corridor.

At the end of the hall they came to electronic doors that opened to a driveway where a car was waiting.

People with cameras were there, and they immediately started snapping pictures. "Oh, no." Annie reached up self-consciously and pushed at her hair. "This is awful."

She glanced down in embarrassment.

"I'm sorry for this," Victor said and stepped up to the large dark vehicle that sat at the curb. A man was waiting and pulled the door open.

Victor slid in and allowed the other person to lift Annie into the car. "Is this the car I hit?" she asked, confused.

"No."

"Is this your car?" was her next question. It was a luxurious car with thick plush seats and a window separating the front from the back.

"Yes."

Annie suddenly had an inkling that this man must have money. No one she knew drove around in a car like this. No one that she knew could afford to. She leaned her head back into the soft seat and sighed as it cupped her sore body. "I guess this was what Cinderella felt like when she got into the coach."

The driver got in and started the vehicle. They drove slowly until they were past the people who were snapping pictures.

He didn't blink at anything that went on, simply sat next to her as they exited the parking lot.

Perhaps the locals always reacted this way? Maybe the ones with cameras had simply been the press wanting pictures of the people in the wreck? A few of the photographers looked awfully young to hold jobs though. But then, she'd heard that people overseas started work younger.

"Where are we going?" she asked when he didn't elaborate about the car or comment on the cameras.

"I live about fifteen minutes outside of town. We'll be there shortly.

"See that valley with the sheep over there?"

Annie followed his finger to where he pointed. "It's beautiful."

"I live about ten kilometers on the other side of it to the east. I have a nice home that's isolated. I raise horses there."

He had to be rich.

Perhaps he was someone important to Holland. "Do you raise tulips?"

The man slowly turned his head and stared at her. His gaze met hers and then touched on her features, causing her cheeks to warm.

Those eyes could hold a person indefinitely. Finally he asked, "Why did you choose Holland to visit?"

It was said kindly, not condemning or rudely. And she felt he was really interested.

"I've heard that it was a beautiful place. I love tulips. And I've always wanted to see a windmill."

"Why did you pick this town?"

"I asked the travel agent for an out-of-the-way place that would be nice to visit. She said there were some famous people who lived here and they had several tourist attractions. Though it was off the beaten path, Europeans liked to frequent it when they visit, she said."

"They do have a nice retreat here," Victor agreed. "About thirty more kilometers north. And they do have a world-famous poet who lives just down the road from me. He's won several honors."

They hit a bump, and Annie winced.

Victor tapped on the window. "Careful, Haufman. Our guest is in pain."

"Yes, sir," the man replied in broken English.

"He speaks English too."

"Yes. Since we're off the main path of tourism you won't meet as many people who speak the language, but there are some. My staff, some do, though others don't. Europeans usually speak several languages."

"Do you speak more than Dutch?"

She shouldn't have asked, but then it seemed so natural.

He nodded his head slightly. "German, Spanish, Italian, Portuguese and a little bit of French, though I understand it much better than I speak it."

"You're kidding." She gasped.

"I have a knack for languages."

She couldn't believe it. "Wow."

"You'll find other people who speak English at the resort and many of the tourist stores. But they're in the northern end of town. As I said, you weren't in a very tourist area. You're lucky anyone right there could understand you."

They turned onto a main road, most likely the

main road she'd been heading for. It wasn't as nice as some she'd driven on in Louisiana but then, there were a few roads in Louisiana that were worse than this as well. This was definitely more populated than the other road. An open market sat on the corner, large and with people hawking their goods. "Oh, look! We have one of those in New Orleans but it's nothing like this."

Victor smiled. "The French Quarter is for show. This one is a working market."

"You've been to New Orleans?"

"On several occasions."

Victor was an enigma. Annie's curiosity was running wild.

"I was going to stay at the resort," she murmured, seeing the buildings they passed. This was definitely not New Orleans.

"I can't see you staying there," Victor murmured.

Suddenly her attention was back on him. How did he manage that? Maybe it was because whenever he spoke it was as if she was hearing a friend. He had a voice that beckoned her to listen.

His voice and certain moves he made seemed familiar. She felt as if she should know him.

Embarrassed that she seemed to be imposing her needs here in Holland on a man she didn't even know, she glanced away. "Why is it that you can't see me staying there?"

"I don't know. You seem more of a woman who would be happier at home surrounded by friends. Maybe one on one."

Well he'd certainly pegged her there. "You're very astute," she replied quietly.

This road wasn't as bumpy, and Annie found herself again relaxing into the thick luxurious seat, though increasingly aware of his presence.

She didn't dare turn and look at Victor. Good heavens. Was she making a mistake staying with him? What had happened to her simple sense of propriety? She wasn't supposed to be attracted to a man. She was a widow!

"You said something about your friends sending you here?"

"No. Yes. Well, no. I mean, I wanted to come. I'm just…well…" She sighed. Still not herself, she probably admitted to more than she should when she elaborated. "I lost my husband four years ago. We'd been married eighteen years when he died. And they thought, for my birthday, they'd give me a trip as a gift. They thought it'd be great for me to get out and see the world before going back to work." She still felt really fuzzy from all the medication. Sleep really sounded nice right now.

"Ah." Victor's voice sounded like an invitation to continue. He leaned back and resumed his regular seat.

Dreamily she said, "It was easier to give in and besides, I think I was actually excited. I already had a passport. And so, a week later I was on the plane."

"On your birthday," he said.

"I told you that?" Annie asked, surprised. Turning her head slowly, she met the caring stare of the man next to her.

"Happy birthday," he murmured and then offered her a slight smile. "You told me quite a bit."

Her cheeks flared with color as she realized she wasn't sure exactly what she'd said. "Oh, dear."

He grinned a large wide grin that lit his eyes, causing them to sparkle with humor. "I'll leave you guessing as to what you told me."

"A gentleman wouldn't do that," Annie said nervously though her eyes drifted half closed. This car was wonderfully comfortable, she thought.

His grin actually widened a bit more. "Now who said I was a gentleman?" And then he laughed. It was a baritone, a deep-throated chuckle.

Not the least bit sexy, but it had the devastating affect of pulling her into the joke and making her want to hear it again.

They passed out of the city and turned east. She

rolled her head toward the window to look out. "The countryside is beautiful. These homes remind me of Heidi."

"Except we don't have mountains. We're below sea level here."

"I remember the story of the boy with his finger in the dike," she said, a languid amusement slipping into her voice.

Small houses sat on parcels of land, and sheep wandered the lush green landscape. "This is beautiful."

"I'm glad you like it. So, do you still want to go home?"

She hesitated. Pulling her gaze from the window, she allowed her vision to travel over to him. "I shouldn't have come in the first place, but the thought of leaving right now..."

He reached out and took her hand in a gentle squeeze. His larger hand engulfed her smaller one. "You're tired and sore. I imagine in the next hour or two the pain medication will be wearing off. This hasn't been the best welcome to our land, but I hope you'll take a day or two and rest before you decide. Then, if you'd like to leave, I'll see you get to the airport."

They turned onto a long drive and Victor glanced out the window. "Here we are," he said.

Annie followed his gaze. She noted the gate that

protected his property. Large with solid round black bars, it kept intruders out. It was more like a fortress, she thought.

The gate opened and they started up the driveway. And then she saw it.

In the distance sat a beautiful two-story chateau surrounded by lush green gardens and green, *green* grass. Nearby were stables and several horses running free.

It looked like a very old house. The gardens and lawns were well-tended and hadn't been put in recently.

"How old is the house?"

"I only bought it about five years ago. It's an escape for me. However, I was told by the Realtor that it's over a hundred and forty years old."

"Relatively new for something in the Old World, isn't it?"

"I'm impressed. Yes, actually it is. I liked the way the land was laid out, the reclusive situation and my mother was from Holland. So I bought it."

He wasn't from here then. No. He was American, wasn't he? She didn't remember if he'd told her that or if she'd just decided it. Yet he spoke the local language well. His mom had probably taught him.

They pulled to a stop in front of the house and

the driver got out. He walked around and opened the door.

"So what are we going to do about getting you inside?" Victor asked as he climbed past her and stepped out of the car.

She glanced down at herself and winced, realizing just how dirty she was. "Maybe you should consider housing me with your horses," she quipped, though half seriously.

"Won't do. It's been a while since I've had company, and I think I'm going to like you, Annie—"

"Hooper."

"Yes. You told me. Annie Hooper. Therefore, housing you in the stables is out of the question. And you certainly can't walk up those stairs. The doctor said to keep off your leg for at least a day." He paused and scratched the bottom of his chin as he studied her.

Slightly embarrassed, she managed to turn and get her legs out of the car. She would simply force herself to walk, she decided. Surely she could, though it was likely her leg was awfully sore.

The driver offered Victor the pair of crutches, but Victor waved them off. "It looks like I'll just have to carry you," he pronounced.

"But—but I'm a size twelve!" Okay, she wore

fourteens too, but she wasn't telling him that. "You can't possibly do that."

"You can't walk up those stairs. The medication—"

"Well, you can't carry me," she insisted.

He shrugged. "You don't think I can do it?"

She gasped as he leaned toward her, and with a strong sure grip, hauled her up into his arms.

Grabbing his neck, she held on.

"Not so tight," he said. "Move them to my shoulders, please."

"I've never been carried before!" She decided to hug him. Leaning forward she moved her arms around his shoulders and buried her head in his neck.

"You were married before," he commented.

"Harry never did this," she said shaking her head.

"Well, then, haven't you ever watched a romantic movie?" he complained.

She groaned.

He chuckled and started toward the stairs. "It looks like I have my work cut out for me."

With that cryptic remark he started up the stairs and into the house where she would be staying for the next few days.

Chapter Three

Picking up a towel, Victor wiped the sweat from his face. He dropped it back over the side of the treadmill and continued walking. "The rest of this week isn't good for me, Sean. How about we put it off until next week—or later?"

Victor reached up and adjusted the earpiece on his ear and then began to swing his arms in tandem with his steps.

"Sure, Jake," Sean said, calling Victor by the name he was better known by: Jake Rivers. "But what is it that has you fobbing me off for later?"

Sean was British and a good friend. They'd both recently worked on their fourth project together. About four months ago actually. They'd been so busy they hadn't seen each other since then. They were going to a movie premiere in two weeks, and they had decided Sean would come up early and spend some time relaxing before they were off to the premiere.

"I have company."

"Oh?"

Victor sighed. "Yes."

He knew a one-word answer wouldn't cut it for his friend.

"Female company?" Sean asked, his accent very pronounced.

Victor changed his accent to match his friend's. "It's not what you think, dear boy," he said dryly.

Sean laughed. "Then what is it? You have a female at your house and you don't want company. Sounds like something is going on to me."

Victor sobered. "I hit her in a head-on collision yesterday."

"Were you injured?"

He heard the concern and knew his friend was worried. So was he, but about his guest not himself. "I'm fine. It wasn't bad on my end, but the lady in question was a tourist and the wreck was my fault. I was avoiding a dog that ran out in front of me. She has a hairline fracture of her leg, according to the doctor, and a concussion."

"So why is she residing in your house?" Sean

asked, obviously wondering why Victor would take in someone he didn't know.

"She doesn't speak the language and is helpless."

"Doesn't speak the language?"

"She's American."

"Nasty Americans," Sean muttered. "Uncultured and abhorrently uneducated when it comes to other languages and cultures."

Victor was used to Sean's attitude and simply ignored his friend. He switched tones and said mildly, "She needed help."

"I say. Let me guess. The defensive tone suggests she's another one of those stunning size threes with long dark hair and beautiful round eyes that usually end up on your arm. You just haven't 'put the moves on her yet,' as you Americans would say."

"You'd be wrong," was all Victor was willing to reply to that blatant attempt to find out information on his guest. "And as I said, though I do find her interesting, I'm not attracted to her." The cross around her neck still bothered him. He had expected the fire-and-brimstone lecture, the condemnation of his job and so on, but she hadn't reacted that way. It had piqued his curiosity. So of course, that was his only interest—not her eyes or hair or anything else…

Sean gave up. "Okay, old chap. Have it your way. I'll try to stay away the rest of the week, but expect me to show up on your doorstep ready for a game of squash and a nice swim in that indoor pool by Monday."

Victor chuckled. "Thanks and see you then." He reached up and disconnected the link.

He then pulled the earpiece off and placed it in a cubbyhole on the treadmill. Glancing down he saw he had less than five minutes to reach his goal and decided he'd done enough for today.

Turning off the machine, he stepped off.

Grabbing his towel and earpiece he headed toward the shower. He dropped both near the sink and stripped off his sweats and T-shirt.

Reaching into the stall, he turned on the shower and waited for the water to heat. Looking down at his abdomen he noted the injury he had received on the job he'd just finished seemed almost completely healed. A large ugly greenish yellow bruise was all that remained from where the wood had caught him unaware as it'd fallen.

Stepping into the shower he allowed the hot water to wash over him. He'd been stiff and sore this morning when he'd gotten up. Working out and then showering was making all the difference in the world.

He grabbed a bar of soap and lathered himself.

He wondered how his guest was faring.

Sean's words about thinking he was attracted to the woman were ridiculous, of course, except that he had found her fascinating.

She'd been hurt and yet still, somehow, she'd come off sounding so innocent and sweet, so very young.

She reminded him of a young girl he'd known in school when he was still a gangly twelve-year-old. He'd been all legs and arms and the opposite sex had never been interested in him. His face had looked like a map of acne and he'd even worn glasses.

How things changed, he thought bemusedly.

Still, one young girl had become his friend back then. They'd been in Australia at the time, one of his many homes. His parents had been missionaries and had moved every few years. They never stayed in one place long.

The young girl had been sweet and had insisted that it didn't matter what others thought. He had to listen to his heart. He had never forgotten her words.

That's how he'd ended up in his present job.

Of course, the young lady probably hadn't meant he should drop out of church in the process, or drift away from his parents. But when he'd chosen his career, his parents had disowned him.

And he'd gone wild in his life to prove a point to them—that he could do what he wanted and if they thought he was going to be wild and go to ruin, then he would.

Except that now he simply lived his life as he did, not in rebellion. He had no idea when the sense of rebellion had left. Or when that life started to seem normal.

Annie Hooper reminded him of another life, another time that had been quieter, a time when he could confide in friends and not worry about it appearing on the gossip shows across the globe.

Perhaps that was why he'd taken Annie in—because of a time she reminded him of. Still, there was the necklace.

When he finished washing, he stepped out of the shower and dried off. He pulled on the pair of jeans and the soft cotton top that were waiting and then combed his long hair.

Slipping in some conditioner and gel, he quickly scrunched it so it would hold the style before grabbing his electric razor and trimming his beard to keep that two-day-old look. He then brushed his teeth.

Slipping on a pair of leather loafers, he headed upstairs to start his day.

Passing the housekeeper he paused. Turning

back around, he asked in Dutch, "Is Miss Hooper up yet?"

"Yes, sir. She was looking through her clothes when I left."

"You didn't stay with her?" he asked.

The housekeeper dropped her gaze. She was in her thirties and lived in a house about five minutes away with her husband who was the gardener here at the chateau. "She doesn't speak the language, and she didn't seem to want my help."

Victor sighed. "She might not act like it, but she is pretty helpless even if she can't understand you."

He paused then added, "Go to the cook, ask her to write a note in English telling Miss Hooper that breakfast is ready, and I'd enjoy the company if she feels up to it. If she does, I'll be glad to help her downstairs." If she doesn't want to use the service elevator, he silently added, thinking most of his guests would never be caught in the service elevator in a chateau.

"Yes, Mr. Rivers." The housekeeper left to do his bidding.

He shook his head and continued down the hall and into the breakfast room.

He usually had coffee and read the paper while he waited for breakfast. After breakfast he painted and then might ride or take some other exercise before lunch. While he was in Holland he was on his own as far as working out. His pérsonal trainer didn't come with him, instead staying in England. He had a separate trainer he contacted when he was at his flat in New York. But here, here was where he could be alone, away from that world and that life—or almost, he thought, as he seated himself and picked up the morning paper.

He'd made the gossip section.

The cook, who bought the paper when she was out shopping each morning, had folded it to that section, just in case he missed it.

The first page of that section had him walking beside a bloody Annie Hooper who sat in a wheelchair as they left the hospital. At least no one could see Annie's face, as she was looking down.

The headline read: Local Accident Wounds Tourist.

Below it was a short article:

Yesterday afternoon just before noon, Haut experienced some excitement of its own as world-renowned Jake Rivers was in a head-on accident with a local tourist.

Seen here in the picture, Mr. Rivers is taking the tourist home. Should we speculate why? Is she really a tourist, or perhaps more?

Marriage bells might just be in the air for this confirmed ladies' man.

"Good grief," Victor muttered. "How did they get wedding bells from a head-on accident?"

He wondered how long before the international gossip rags picked up the story. He would have to alert security to keep a closer watch on the house. Usually the media left him alone here in Haut but then, usually he didn't have stories like this appearing in the local paper.

Tossing the paper aside, he lifted the silver pot that was warm to touch from the hot brew the cook had recently put into it, and poured himself a cup of coffee.

The sound of scuffling made him pause, and he lifted his gaze toward the door.

Annie Hooper came into sight on her crutches. Looking a bit out of breath she flashed him a sweet smile. "Good morning."

She looked gorgeous today. Actually, he was quite stunned by how pretty she was. He hadn't really noticed yesterday.

She wore a cotton dress that dropped to midcalf and buttoned down the front. It was light green with a belt to match. It was simple, yet suited her.

Her hair was pulled up and pinned at the back of her head. The hairstyle did not do her justice.

It looked as if she'd applied makeup, because, as he studied the bruise on her forehead, he noted it wasn't as dark as it should be. He could see the stitches from here with the way she wore her hair.

She was barefoot and not wearing stockings.

Quickly setting down the coffeepot, he stood. "I would have come up and assisted you," he said as he started toward her. "Didn't Helena tell you that?"

"Who?" Annie asked, breathing heavily as she rested on the crutches.

"Helena, the housekeeper who has been assisting you. She was bringing you a note to that effect since she doesn't speak English."

"I haven't seen her. Perhaps I left before she got up there?" She asked it gently as if she thought she might have done something wrong.

"It's okay," he assured her.

Victor walked with her to the table and then pulled out a chair for her.

"Thank you," she said. "These take a while to get the hang of, you know. I've never broken a bone before."

"How do you feel today?"

The look she sent him was one he completely understood. "That bad, huh?"

She chuckled and then winced. "The air bag didn't deploy in my car. I don't even think it had one. My chest is bruised as are the front of my hips from the steering wheel and seat belt, I suppose. And I saw myself in the mirror this morning. My forehead is blue—and I'm sure that blue runs up to the top of my head where it's very tender. My shoulders and my lower back—are also very sore.''

He took the crutches and rested them against the table next to her chair, before turning it so she could easily slide into it. ''I can help you a bit there,'' he said and slipped his hand to her back to help ease her down. His hand moved up to her shoulder and rested there a minute in sympathy for her injuries. With a gentle squeeze, he released her.

Going around to his chair, he seated himself. ''I asked the cook to make a regular American breakfast. I hope that's okay. It should be here shortly. Would you like some coffee?''

She was seated directly to his left. A plate was laid out for her, just in case she had decided to eat. If not, it would be taken up after breakfast. His staff was used to him having guests and had a routine for such occasions. Though he rarely had more than two or three people here at a time, he did make sure he had a staff that knew how to set up for parties.

''Yes, coffee sounds fine.''

He poured her a cup.

She smiled shyly and nodded. "How are you feeling?"

"Much better after working out and taking a nice hot shower."

"You went to a gym already this morning?" she asked, her eyes showing amazement.

He shook his head. "Not at all. There's a kitchen and gym in the basement. If you didn't notice when we drove in, stairs lead up to the first floor, which is actually the second floor. We call the basement our first floor. The second floor, which in reality is the third floor, houses the bedrooms and then this floor, the second, which we call the first, is for entertaining and such."

"Nice," she said and then shook her head and started laughing. "Remind me never to ask you for directions."

He chuckled, realizing he'd confused her and silently admitting he just might have done it on purpose to pull a smile from her.

"We don't have a real basement because of the low land. At any rate, you're welcome to use the workout equipment if you'd like. Attached to the northeast corner of the house is my studio. You'll note the floor has a decline you walk down to get to it. If you feel up to a tour later, I'll show it to you. At the bottom of the decline there's another section that was built on later. It was probably supposed to be a separate bedroom, but I turned it into a painting studio. There's an inside hothouse for fresh vegetables located there, and then off that is a pool area. It's enclosed with glass so you can look out at the landscape as you swim, but heated, since I'm used to warmer weather.''

"I'm used to much warmer weather," Annie said lightly and smiled.

"I would imagine, being from Louisiana."

"I told you that too?"

He nodded, amused at how her eyes sparkled.

"I don't remember much at all from yesterday," she confessed.

Now she seemed closer to forty than twenty. The blushes of yesterday had seemed so young for her. The knowing look in her eyes bespoke someone older, someone who had a bit of experience. She was so dichotomous.

"I would ask what is on your mind, but then, I'm not sure I want to know the answer."

Victor chuckled. "I was thinking you finally make me feel safe."

"Safe?" she asked and tilted her head slightly.

"Yesterday I was worried about letting you stay here. In some ways you seemed very young. Today, however, I can see the maturity of a woman."

Her cheeks bloomed with color as her gaze cut away. She actually swallowed.

"I didn't mean to say something wrong," he said gently, having no idea what he'd said to cause her to react the way she had.

"You didn't. It's just…" She glanced back. "I don't think anyone has ever said such a beautiful thing that made me feel so feminine."

He threw back his head and laughed. "Annie, you amuse me."

He was saved from explaining that by one of his staff bringing in breakfast. Fresh fruits and cereal as well as scrambled eggs and cheese covered the two trays.

"I hope you don't expect me to eat half of this," Annie said, her eyes widening in surprise at the amount of food brought to the table.

"Not at all. Eat what you'd like. I wasn't sure what you might enjoy so I asked the cook to provide several things. And we always have cheese, at every meal in some form or another. Holland is known for her cheeses."

"I didn't know that."

He pointed to a wedge and said, "Try that."

Obediently she picked up the tongs and lifted a piece of cheese onto her plate.

Victor served some eggs, cheese and fruit onto his plate and watched as Annie picked up the piece of cheese and nibbled it. Lifting her eyebrows she glanced at him. "It's very good."

He nodded. "Cook knows my tastes. I'm glad you like it as well."

To his utter surprise, Annie Hooper bowed her head and moved her lips silently.

He hadn't seen someone do that in…he couldn't remember the last time. Probably before he left home. He'd almost forgotten the cross necklace, which she wasn't wearing today.

When she was done she looked up.

He quickly glanced away so she wouldn't know he'd been staring. Dichotomous indeed. She was nice, not condemning, gentle, not harsh…. "I plan to do some painting later today. However, if you feel up to a tour, I'd much rather show you the house."

At her gasp he glanced back at her.

"Ah, the paper." She had spotted the picture of the two of them on the front page of the society section.

Obviously, she'd never been in the paper before, which caused him to wonder what she was going to say if she made news back in the States. "The local paper thrives on excitement. A head-on crash is something that doesn't often happen in our small town."

"The paper is in Dutch."

He nodded. "You can find papers from Amsterdam in English, but out here, it's a matter of pride.'' He got up and crossed the wooden floor to the sideboard and picked up the morning Amsterdam paper. ''You can read this if you'd like.''

She silently accepted the paper.

He was amazed that she didn't recognize him. Amazed and a bit disturbed, he realized. The second shamed him a bit, but then, he was so used to being known and this woman didn't show the least bit of evidence of recognition. Even seeing them together in the paper hadn't triggered anything. And as much as he wanted to explain, he found he really didn't want to either. If he brought out things like that, then she most likely would act differently and he wanted to be with her like this, just like a normal person who could relive some of the past for a while. His pride could take a beating. It felt rather refreshing, actually, the more he thought about it.

Would she have prayed in front of him had she known the truth?

He admitted the prayer had made him uncomfortable. How long had it been since he'd prayed? How long had it been since he'd been in church? Too long, he acknowledged, but then, he'd done so many things, changed so much that he doubted he would even be welcomed by God, though he was certain most would welcome him into the congregation, for the ability to say they knew him.

Realizing the cynical turn of his thoughts, he mentally changed direction. He wasn't a little boy anymore, intimidated by his parents and forced to go to church, though he again remembered that young girl of so long ago, a daughter of some other missionaries in the area. He'd made friends with her until his parents had found out what her parents believed and forbidden him to be around them.

His parents had been so very negative, he thought now. Over the years he'd met a few people who said they were Christians, but then, they went out and socialized just like him, so he had to wonder. While he found Annie refreshing, he was still cynical. He would simply keep his thoughts to himself on the subject.

He began to eat.

"I think I'd like a tour very much," Annie murmured as she finished glancing through the paper.

At her smile he asked, "What is it?"

"This is so different from an American paper."

"Just wait until you see the TV," he said.

Her eyes widened. "I hadn't thought about that."

"Many shows are in English with Dutch subtitles so you can actually watch some of them if you'd like."

"Holland is so industrialized compared to what I'd expected."

Victor laughed. "We are major exporters to other countries. The tulips and windmills and serene countryside are tourist attractions, but we do live in the twenty-first century."

"Sometimes I think Americans aren't well educated about other places," she said idly as she scanned the paper.

"A great disservice the school systems do to their children."

She nodded. "My children didn't learn a lot about world geography or world history."

"You have children?" he asked, surprised. He hadn't thought about that, but she was a widow and forty years old.

She smiled. "Yes, well, not exactly. They're older now, but they are my husband's children."

"You've never had children?"

She shook her head. "And you?"

The food turned dry in his mouth. "I have a thirteen-year-old son. He's with my ex-wife right now."

"Divorced?"

He nodded and thought, here comes the lecture. "We were married two years. When Josh was a year old, she decided she didn't like being with me and left. Josh lives with me about six months of every year. I should be getting him again in a few weeks."

"How does he handle that?"

No lecture. Interesting, he thought. "He's used to it. I normally would have him most of the summer but it didn't work out that way this summer. I sometimes wish he was living here with me."

"Divorce is hard on children. My husband's children never got over it, and they used their parents against each other."

He felt sad at the thought of this woman as a young girl dealing with something like that. "Josh hasn't tried that. But I think he's unhappy lately." Victor sighed. "At any rate, he's the pride of my life."

Finishing up their breakfast in silence, he waited until she'd patted her lips and removed her napkin from her lap before asking, "Would you like a tour now, or would you prefer to wait?"

He'd seen her slip some pills out of one of her pockets and take them at breakfast and hoped those were pain medications.

"I'm actually feeling much better. If you're game, let's go."

He stood and came around to her side where he pulled out the chair. Annie struggled to her feet and reached for her crutches, but with her cast, she slipped. She gasped and fell forward, arms flailing as she grabbed for the chair but couldn't find her balance.

Victor leapt forward just in time, catching her in his arms. Her soft warm body thudded into his harder one and he stood braced, accepting the weight and pulling her into the safety of his strength.

Annie clung to him, working to get her balance. He waited, allowing her time to recover. While he did, he noted again that she smelled of the oddly sweet fragrance he'd caught a scent of yesterday. He smelled it in her hair as her head brushed his cheek, or perhaps it was on her neck.

He wanted to lean down and inhale again, but she chose that moment to look up.

Their gazes met, and he realized he still held her. He hadn't let her go. Suddenly he became conscious of the fact that he was attracted to this woman.

Sean had been right.

Though he hadn't recognized it originally, he now admitted that he found this woman very attractive. How had that happened?

She studied his eyes and her hands, against his chest, flexed slightly. Then she smiled and said, nervously, "We've got to stop meeting like this."

Some perverse imp in him didn't let her off the hook as a gentleman should. Instead, he smiled and replied, "Oh, I don't know, I kinda like this."

Chapter Four

"Telephone, Mr. Rivers."

The spell was broken, thank goodness. At least for her—sort of.

"Take a message," he told the woman who stood there.

"It's your son," the maid said hesitantly, but then added, "still, I'll tell him to call back."

"Wait, no." Victor hesitated, his eyes touching Annie's eyes, her cheeks, her lips and then, with what seemed reluctance to Annie, he loosened his hold. "I'll take the call."

He dropped his arms from around her and stepped back from Annie. She found she could breathe again now that Victor's strong arms weren't distracting her from it.

''If you'll excuse me for a moment, Helga will start the tour and I'll catch up.''

''Not at all.'' She took the crutches he offered and slipped them under her arms.

He paused to cast one last inscrutable glance her way and then strode from the room.

Oh, heavens, she thought, collapsing in relief against the crutches. She knew desire when she felt it, and that was what was thrumming along every nerve ending in her body.

She was attracted to Victor Rivers.

Parts of her that she had thought had died with Harry obviously weren't dead at all. This was different however. She could remember being all starry-eyed when she'd met Harry so many years ago, but this…how could she explain it?

This was not that starry-eyed attraction of a young girl. It was an attraction of a grown woman who knew about relationships between a man and a woman and understood how much more went into them.

She found her hands were actually shaking with reaction and couldn't believe it.

Attraction.

To a man who she'd only just met.

She had to be crazy.

It had to be something in the air.

Or something she'd ingested.

"Ma'am."

She was losing it. *Dear Father, what am I supposed to do?*

"Ma'am?"

Annie glanced up.

The young maid smiled. "I give tours quite often. If you'll follow me. Mr. Rivers, he is very proud of his house."

Annie smiled, readjusted her crutches and nodded. "It is a beautiful house of which to be proud."

She thought of the look in Victor's eyes as he'd held her. She was almost certain he was attracted to her as well.

Wiping her moist palms on her skirt, she gripped the crutches. "Lead the way," she murmured. "I can't wear any pantyhose because of this cast and so I couldn't wear my shoes. I hope Mr. Rivers doesn't mind," she said as Helga started down the hall.

The maid didn't answer. Instead she pointed out a painting. "A masterpiece, this art, he recently acquired."

Real, Annie thought, not a reprint. *Wow!*

And thus started the tour. As she walked, Annie managed to convince herself that she was reading meanings into Victor's actions that just weren't there. That had to be the explanation. She was forty, had grown kids and had never been out of Louisiana. She was simply putting her feelings and needs onto him. But, oh, around him, she didn't feel forty. She said that as if it meant she was old. She found she didn't feel old at all, but very young.

The house was beautiful. Wooden floors in some rooms and carpeted floors in others. Mahogany items that looked older than the house itself, yet which shone with a beauty that bespoke daily polishing dotted the hallways and rooms. However, despite the house's beauty, with the paintings and sculptures and decorated walls, it was devoid of any personal items. She did not see a single picture of Victor or of his son. Where was the home in the house?

By the time they were approaching the ramp that led to the lower part of the house, Victor returned. He dismissed the maid and then slowed his pace to walk beside Annie.

"You're disturbed," she began and slowed her gait. "Perhaps I can finish the tour later."

"No." He hesitated and then turned toward her and offered her a gallant smile, albeit a short one. "It was the conversation with my son on the phone."

He actually bowed slightly, motioning her on ahead.

She complied. Though she knew it wasn't her

business, she ventured into dangerous territory. "Problems?"

He sighed. "He wants to come and visit now."

She wondered what the problem was. They continued on in silence until he added, "His mother won't let him for a few more weeks."

"I see."

"I don't," Victor said, frustration rife in his voice. He clenched his hands and then relaxed them, releasing a long breath. "I don't know what is going on with Josh. He's unhappy, that's all I know. He won't tell me why. He just says he wants to fly to Holland and stay with me."

Annie asked carefully, "You don't think he's in danger, do you?"

"What?" He glanced up sharply then shook his head, his hair moving about his face. "No. Not at all. I mean, I would think I could tell that. He sounds more upset than scared. I thought about flying up there and settling this, but Josh doesn't want me to do that."

They approached a doorway and Victor stepped forward to open it for her. "Perhaps," Annie began as she maneuvered into the room, "simply calling him often and talking with him might alleviate any frustration he has and help him make it through until he can come visit."

Light and airy, the room had white walls and a

lot of windows. It even had a door that led outside.
You could see tulips along with many other flowers and bushes outside. It was breathtaking and Annie could see why Victor would use this as a room
to paint.

Easels and canvas, along with paints and rags,
lay about the room. There was a smell of paint
cleaner of some sort and oil paints.

Two old leather chairs and a small table were
off in one corner and two bookcases with books,
loose-leaf paper and pens were also there.

Victor smiled. "You're right. Calling him more
might just be the perfect solution."

Annie returned his smile, feeling at home with
this man as they talked. The attraction was still
there, underneath everything, but simply talking
with him touched her just as much. "You have a
great relationship with your son, I take it?"

He nodded. "We get along wonderfully. I miss
him when he's not around."

"I wish Harry had worked at a relationship like
that with his children," she said and sighed.

"Your former husband?" Victor asked.

She nodded. "I was convinced I was so in love
when I met him. He was a nice man and had just
gone through a terrible divorce. He was never close
to them, a workaholic. It was very hard on them."

"And on you, it sounds," Victor murmured.

Surprised she glanced at him. "No. I don't think so. I never knew anything else. He married me and took me into his house. I raised his kids. He provided for me. He was a good man."

"But did he love you?" Victor asked, then dropped his head slightly, abashed. "I'm sorry. That's none of my business."

Annie answered anyway. "I was only seventeen, a senior in high school. I married into an instant family and never had time to slow down." She paused, considering. "I could have done a lot worse. He never mistreated me, and I did care for him." She smiled, for what she said was true.

Victor reached up and touched her shoulder. "There's much more to many relationships than that."

She felt his touch and shivered, thinking, yes, she could believe that after meeting this man.

She glanced around the room, casting about for an excuse to change the subject. Victor followed her gaze. She stopped on his painting that was in progress. "I like the colors. What are you making?"

"I'm trying to create peace. Thus far, I don't think I've quite caught it."

She looked at the dark colors and frowned. "I'd think peace would be lighter."

He shrugged. "Perhaps for some."

"I'm going to be teaching art at the community center starting in August. That's why I took eight weeks off to tour Holland."

"Eight weeks?"

"Well, I only planned to stay two weeks, since the kids are so upset about me being gone. But my ticket is open-ended—my friends insisted I do it that way."

"So, you're an artist too?" he asked.

"Oh, no." She laughed self-consciously. "I didn't mean to give that impression. I love art and have always wanted to paint, but I've just never had the time."

He grinned. "Yet you will be teaching art?"

She shrugged. "They said I needed no experience. They're simply desperate for someone to fill the job, and I was tired of staying at home and wanted something to occupy my days."

"I have an idea." Victor strode away from her and across the room to where another easel was located. He set the painting that was displayed on it on the floor and lifted the easel from its corner. Bringing it back across the room, he placed it in an empty spot near the window. He then crossed to the other side of the room and grabbed a large empty canvas and returned with it, putting it upon the easel. "Why don't I give you some lessons over the next few days while you're here recovering?''

Shocked and surprised she said, ''You'd do that?''

He grinned. ''I love to paint and would enjoy your company in the mornings while I'm working. My son often sits in here and paints with me when he's around.''

''I feel like I'm putting you out,'' Annie said quietly, despite the fact that she was flattered that he seemed to have accepted her presence.

He sighed. Lifting both hands in frustration he said, ''Why can't you see, Annie, that you've ended an ennui in me. You've given me a chance to live again within the real world instead of the reclusive world I've exiled myself to this past month. Your presence will be a potion to heal my afflicted soul. I need you, Annie.''

Annie simply stared a heartbeat before she burst into laughter. ''Okay, okay. But I didn't come to Holland to sit in someone's house. When I get better I insist on moving to the lodge and doing some sightseeing.''

''You don't have to be better to sightsee. I'll be glad to take you to the real sites, not the silly little tourist sites.''

''Will you be driving?'' Annie asked, teasingly.

Victor's face broke into a wide grin. "Not if you don't want me to."

Her smile faded. "I feel like I am imposing upon you. Can't I do something to repay you for all of this kindness?"

She really meant what she said, but his response was something she hadn't expected. "Just be my friend for the time you're here, Annie Hooper. Simply be yourself and talk with me, and I'll be the happiest man in Haut."

This man, with all of his money, with his child, with his hobbies, was a lonely man. That disturbed her.

Though he smiled and laughed, though he was tender and gentle and a kickback to an era when men were actually gentlemen, he was lonely.

Did he realize it, she wondered?

And she wondered if he was a Christian.

If he wasn't, then perhaps she could help him find the cure to his loneliness.

"There's something else I want to do for you while you're here, if you're interested."

She smiled as Victor placed a stool before the easel and motioned her over. "And what is that?" she asked archly as she made her way to the stool.

He took the crutches from her and steadied her as she seated herself.

"I'd like to teach you Dutch."

Surprised, she gawked. "You're kidding?"

He shook his head. Returning with a paint-covered shirt, he handed it to her. "Slip this on over your dress so you don't soil it." He pulled on an oversize shirt and rolled the sleeves to his elbows. As he did, he continued, "We could do simple things like colors and phrases. It'd be a great learning experience for you. And think how that would impress your friends back home."

She thought this guy would impress them much more than a few Dutch words. "I'm not sure how good I am at languages. I mean, you speak so many."

He shrugged. "You won't know if you don't try."

That sounded like a challenge to her. "I can try," she said and smiled.

"Good. *Rood,*" he said and pointed.

She looked down at where his finger was. "Paints?" she asked.

"No. That means red." He went from color to color as he started squeezing them out on her palette. *"Rood, oranje, groen, geel, blauw."*

She tried to repeat them. *"Rood, oranje, grung…"*

"Groen and blauw. Green and blue."

"Gr-oen and…blauw."

"Geel," he said gently for yellow.

"Geel."

"No. Put your tongue like this and let it simply roll off."

She tried. It didn't work.

He grinned. Coming around behind her he nestled up until his front was to her back. "We'll work on the names as we paint."

Leaning forward he picked up the paint-daubed palette. He reached around her with both arms. "Let's put this on your hand to start with. If you get tired, you can lay it down. Don't worry about what we do today, I'm just going to teach you some strokes and things about different brushes. I put out samples of some of the basic colors so we can have fun with them and so it won't be boring as we learn, okay?"

"Sure." She was having trouble concentrating. Again she realized just how physical this man was. Neither Harry nor the children were very physical beings. Her mom had been. Her dad hadn't, though more so than Harry. But Victor seemed to touch all of the time.

He currently surrounded her on three sides. It made her want to relax and simply enjoy his presence. She sighed as her body relaxed against his. She'd missed companionship, she thought and really liked this.

"You have the palette comfortably in your hand?"

She nodded and could feel his chin brush the side of her head. He began explaining about the different brushes, and one by one he picked them up and positioned them in her hand. He showed her how to hold them, what each one was used for and encouraged her to try different colors as she learned how to wield her weapon, as he'd called it.

But best of all, he made her laugh. It didn't take long for her to become accustomed to him. They were having fun as they tried different colors and different strokes of the brushes. At one point he moved away from her to gather his own brushes. When he returned to her side, he wielded his own brush, showing her the differences and helping guide her through her learning experience.

She thought this was probably the best time she could remember having had in the last several years. And she thanked God that she was here to enjoy it.

All things truly did work out. Had she not been questioning God about life lately and whether this was all? And He had blessed her with this wonderful experience and this wonderful man to share it with.

As they continued laughing and painting, she didn't think life could get much better.

Chapter Five

❧

"Oh, my! This is wonderful!"

The blindfold removed, Annie stood in front of the dinner table regarding Victor's efforts.

He'd had such a wonderful time today with Annie. In fact he couldn't remember the last time he'd had that much fun. She was wonderful and different from other women he'd met. He couldn't explain it. She had an inward glow about her constantly and her gentle words were so lighthearted and innocent compared to how jaded he'd become.

So he'd planned a special dinner with her. The table was set formally with two places. Candles were lit, and hanging on the wall was the painting the two of them had created earlier today.

"Our picture!" she squealed in delight.

He grinned. "I just had to hang it. I had it framed today while you were resting." It was really a mess with no true patterns, but it represented something special to him, with bright bold colors in vivid strokes next to smaller, tentative strokes.

"You shouldn't have!" she exclaimed, but her happiness was obvious in her eyes.

He slipped his arm around her and lifted her own arm to his shoulders. Guiding her to the chair next to his, he seated her. "I did because I want always to be reminded of the good time we had today. At least, I had a good time."

"Oh, so did I. Who would have believed coming to Holland would fulfill one of my lifelong dreams—to learn about painting?"

He couldn't explain how her enthusiasm affected him. Releasing her, he allowed his hand to travel down her arm and catch her hand; he squeezed gently. "I'm very honored that you enjoyed it."

"And thank you for this wonderful dinner. Do you always eat so formally?"

He grinned. "We won't tomorrow or Sunday. I always give my employees the weekend off—at least my house employees," he amended, thinking that security was never off. "So then it's usually sandwiches." He returned to his own seat.

"Well this is nice, and I am perfectly fine with fixing a sandwich to eat."

Just then Helga brought in the first course of the meal—a lightly flavored cheese soup. She set the dishes down and left.

Annie bowed her head and silently prayed before tasting the soup. He waited uncomfortably until she was done and then lifted his spoon. "So, what do you think?" he asked when she tasted it, wondering how, as a Christian, she could be so different from what his experience of Christians had previously been. She showed love, not judgment. Gentleness without compromise, yet without condemnation.

Her eyes were closed and a smile spread across her face. She looked as if she were in rapture. "This is absolutely wonderful," she said in utter delight. "You have the best cook in the world."

"I'm sure she'll enjoy hearing that," he said dryly. "And I'm sure she'll be asking for a raise right after I tell her what you said."

Annie laughed. It was an unencumbered laugh, full of joy and life. "You're too funny," she said lightly and took another taste.

Victor began his own soup, thinking that though it was good, it did not compare to watching Annie when she was happy. Her smile was nourishment to his dry and empty soul. What was it he'd heard once? A person doesn't know their soul is dry and empty until someone comes along who can expose it.

Annie was the key to his emptiness. Her laughter and joy put a hunger in him for that experience.

Until not too long ago he would have said life was fine. Sure he had gotten burned out more often lately, and he was spending more time at his house here in Holland, which was his escape-from-life house, but that was because of his job—or so he'd thought.

Annie.

She took another spoonful of soup, and he watched as her eyes sparkled. "I think I've got that big fuzzy brush down," she said, describing, badly, one of the painting brushes, "but that tiny one is going to be a problem."

She wasn't aware of how animated she was as she moved her spoon in circles explaining about the brushes.

"It will come with practice." Lot's of practice, he thought. She'd kept getting carried away and making funny uncontrolled strokes when he'd been trying to teach her control today.

He wondered if she was always so animated. The way she'd talked earlier had led him to believe that she wasn't. He didn't think she had ever had a chance to cut loose and have fun. He got the feeling she had lived a very sheltered life with no time for herself—until now.

He loved watching her come to life. Yesterday

and this morning before the painting, she'd been a bit reserved, but now, she was much more open.

"So you said you'd never painted before, but did you have any art lessons?" he asked, trying to draw out more information.

She shook her head. "I've tried my hand at drawing and writing poetry, but with the kids, I never had time for lessons."

"It sounds as if they took up a lot of your time."

"I never had a moment for myself," she said, oblivious to how that sounded. "As they got older I was always running them everywhere. I still do my son's laundry. He's thirty-three-plus and drops by once a week. I do laundry, and he and I sit and talk."

"About what?" he queried, frowning slightly. Thirty-three and he still brought his laundry to his stepmom to do? The man should be taken out and told the basics of life. He himself had done his own laundry from about twelve onward.

"Usually his work. He'll tell me what's going on in his work and what he's hoping to accomplish. He has his Ph.D. and works at a local chemical plant where he designs analysis for quality control purposes."

"What did he say when you told him you were coming to Holland?" he queried mildly as the maid brought in their salads.

"Well, he wasn't happy," she replied and took a sip of her water.

He lifted his glass to his lips and sipped, watching as Annie's features changed slightly from animated back to the reserved, tired-looking woman of this morning. "He didn't think it was very responsible of me to take off so soon after his dad's death."

"It's been four years," Victor said and then regretted it. He didn't want to put her on the defensive.

"I told you that too, huh?" She looked as if she was trying to remember what she'd told him and then shrugged. "My son was certain I'd come over here and go crazy and blow all of the money Harry left to me. It wasn't much by today's standard, but if I'm frugal, I can make it last the rest of my life."

Frugal.

In other words, Harry hadn't left her a lot of money and the kids were worried she was going to blow it all, leaving them nothing. He was beginning to see a picture painted of Annie's life that he didn't like.

He reminded himself he wanted to enjoy her company, but how could one simply enjoy a person's company if one didn't expand one's knowledge about that person? She was so open and innocent, sharing what many people certainly wouldn't share with someone they barely knew. But that was just Annie.

"Susan, my daughter, is a nurse and she thought it was simply wrong of me to leave. I have a house and a cat, what more did I need?"

A life, Victor wanted to say, but he refrained.

"My friends thought I had mourned long enough and said 'go for it.' They thought it'd be nice for me to get away."

"And they were right," he said, thinking he should send her friends thank you gifts for allowing Annie a break. "You've already had some Dutch lessons and now painting lessons."

The maid brought in small Cornish hens that had been cooked with rosemary. "How do you say chicken in Dutch?" she asked staring at the golden-brown hen.

"Kip," he said slowly and carefully, pronouncing it so she could hear the sounds.

"Kip," she repeated slowly.

He nodded. "Very good," he said.

She picked up her water glass again and took a sip.

He frowned, noting she wasn't drinking her wine. "Is the wine not to your liking?"

She blinked. "Oh. No. That's not it at all. You see, I don't drink."

"Ah." He should have realized. Here it comes,

the lecture. "I suppose you don't want me drinking?" he asked, opening the door for her rebuke.

"Oh, I don't care," she replied and she was so honest about it, he believed her.

"Well that's a first," he muttered. Too late he realized the breech he'd made. He never discussed his past with anyone, and yet he'd just opened the door to her.

"A first?" she asked, and glanced at him.

He didn't want to say anything, but, for some reason, so many memories of his past were opened just by having her around him. They were always near the surface when she was present. Giving in to the subject change that he'd inadvertently caused, he said simply as he began tearing apart the hen, "My parents were missionaries. They preached no alcohol whatsoever, and I haven't met a Christian yet who doesn't lecture me on my drinking."

"Well, perhaps they should get a life."

She'd surprised him again.

"You don't mind drinking?" he asked, suddenly very curious about her attitude toward drinking.

"I didn't say that."

Ah-ha, he thought.

"Actually, in the Bible, Paul told Timothy to drink some wine. Jesus made wine. I don't suppose drinking is wrong per se. However, I think if you have alcoholics in the family, if you feel a convic-

tion in your heart that it's wrong, or if you tend
toward drunkenness, then, no, you shouldn't drink.
But if you have no problem with it and you don't
go out driving, or beating your wife or children,
then I don't see a problem with it.''

''Why don't you drink?'' he asked, unable not
to delve deeper.

''I don't think it's right for me. I fear I would
overindulge, and frankly, I feel it displeases my
heavenly Father.''

''Your father,'' he said having never heard anyone talk quite like that about God.

She chuckled and even blushed slightly. ''Yeah.
Well, I was taught that God loved me so much that
He sent His Son, and because of that He says we
are joint heirs with Jesus. So, that makes God my
father. And better yet, that makes Jesus my big
brother.''

''I've never heard that before.'' He liked the
way she blushed and looked so absolutely innocent
and young when she said that.

''But your parents were missionaries,'' she said.
He heard the confusion in her voice and saw the
bewilderment in her eyes.

''Yes. But they talked repentance and sin.''

''Well that is certainly part of it,'' she said, nodding and he suddenly wondered how he had gotten
into this conversation. ''I mean the Bible is fact
and it tells us that every one of us have strayed

from the Truth. That's why God sent His Son. To bring us back in line with that Truth. By accepting Jesus's sacrifice for our straying and admitting that we've strayed, we are cleaned up from those past mistakes. His blood now takes the place of our penalty. But that's only the beginning. What God wants is a relationship. That's why He sent His Son. He could have given up on us as soon as Adam sinned, but He knew from the foundations of the world what was going to happen and provided a way out for us. And you know what is so wonderful?'' she asked, and the soft smile of joy that touched her features made it worth listening to her just to see that expression. ''We don't have to do anything for that sacrifice except say yes.''

He'd heard it before, but never that way. It'd always been about how bad a person was and how, if they didn't repent, they'd end up in hell. This was different. She talked about God sending His Son out of love, not out of condemnation of the human race followed with threats or fears. For him it'd been all rules and regulations, for her it was something different.

He was having his conceptions turned upside down by this woman.

''I did that once—a long time ago,'' he finally admitted. ''But it turned sour on me and I'm not into the religion thing anymore.''

''Well that's good,'' she said.

"Good? But aren't you a Christian?" he asked bewildered by her statement.

She nodded. "Yes, Victor, I am. But I'm not into religion. As I said, I'm into a relationship with Jesus. He talks to me. I talk to Him. I share things with Him."

"You don't go to church?" She had confused him this time.

"Yes, I do. And I'd like to go this Sunday if possible. But that's not what a relationship is about. You go to church for fellowship and to learn."

"Let's change the subject," Victor said, unnerved by such a different vision of religion from that he'd always perceived.

She smiled. "So tell me, when do I get to see a windmill?"

His mind whirled. He had expected an argument from her, and yet, she hadn't said a word. She was really something else. He was actually off balance. "How about Monday? That way you'll have the weekend to rest."

Wiping his fingers on the napkin, he waited patiently allowing the maid to take the main course and set down dessert.

"Really?" she asked. "I mean, I was only kidding. I honestly don't expect you to be my tour guide, though I have to admit, today was one of the best days I've had in my life."

He chuckled and simply shook his head. "It would be my pleasure, Annie, to take you on a tour of the countryside and show you the windmills and even a few beautiful fields of tulips if you'd like."

She smiled. "Do you know, that's one of the reasons I chose Holland for a vacation? I love tulips. They're my favorite flower. Harry preferred roses, but I always cherished a secret longing for tulips. Not the multi-colored ones, but the solid-colored beautiful flowers."

He watched the dreamy look on her face as she discussed tulips and was entranced.

"My favorite colors are blue and pink and yellow. Well, almost any of them. I imagine if I found a really pretty multi-colored one I'd like it as well."

"Do you plant them where you live?"

"No. I'm not a gardener. I tend to kill plants. All plants. Even houseplants." She gave him a mournful sigh before taking a bite of the soufflé. Then she perked up. "I *really* think you should give your cook a raise."

He burst into rich laughter. This woman was a pleasure. She kept him unbalanced in a world where he was always balanced and in control.

"I'll see about it."

They finished their desserts in silence. When

they were done, Victor stood and strode to Annie to assist her from her chair.

She rose to her feet, without a repeat of this morning's stumble, much to Victor's dismay. He wouldn't have minded having her fall into his arms again. Third time, they say, is a charm. He motioned toward the sitting room. "I'd like to hear about the poetry you write. I also write poetry."

Surprised, Annie looked at the man beside her. "You're kidding. Is there anything you don't do?"

"I don't play football, that's soccer to you, or American football for that matter. Nor can I grow plants."

"Ah-ha. You're not perfect. I was beginning to wonder." And she was. As far as she was concerned, he *was* perfect—except for his relationship with Christ. Someone had hurt him in his past.

He was pretty closed to the gospel, and unfortunately that was probably what his problem was. If he was unwilling to let Christ in to heal his heart, then he wasn't going to find the peace he was searching for.

That concerned her. However, she thought perhaps God had allowed her to be here to minister to this man. Nothing ever happened that wasn't in God's control, though she often wondered about that sometimes when bad things happened. She had to rely on the fact that God could see the entire picture and she couldn't. She had wondered sometimes why Harry had died so young. One day in heaven she would ask God. And if she didn't ever find out why she'd ended up here in this man's house, she just might ask Him about that too.

Still, the fact remained that Victor was hurting, and she could help him—maybe. So what would it hurt to stay here for a while? He'd offered her the comfort of his house and his services as tour guide.

She certainly could have done worse. She most likely would have been lonely by now, sitting in the hotel all by herself.

Instead she was enjoying herself more than she had in eons and actually learning some new things in the process. She felt alive again.

Could things get any better than this?

She hadn't thought so at breakfast, but here they were at dinner, going into the parlor to talk about poetry.

She had a feeling she was going to be up way past her bedtime.

And she found she didn't mind.

Chapter Six

Annie was in the depths of burgeoning guilt. How could she have forgotten to call Mark and Susan until last night? They were upset that she wasn't at the lodge. She explained that she'd met a nice American who was allowing her to stay in a château—she didn't mention the American was a man—and they'd gotten even angrier. Mark had insisted that she couldn't stay with someone she didn't know. The people might kill her in her sleep—she didn't tell them he was alone except for his staff, either. Susan said that she was there to see the countryside, not make friends with strange people who might be after her money.

They both suggested she consider coming home early.

She was glad she hadn't told them about her accident.

She hadn't given them the phone number, promising to find out what it was and call them back the next day with it.

When she'd hung up, all of the joy of the day had evaporated. She had thought to share more with them about learning to paint and the wonderful dinner, but it hadn't worked out that way.

Saturday she and Victor had stayed around the house and painted as well as worked on her Dutch. She'd spent a lot of time resting, the exhaustion from her accident catching up with her. And she'd spent a lot of time feeling a connection developing between her and Victor. To say she was attracted to this man was an understatement. She was fascinated with everything he said, deriving joy from simply being with him, and when he touched her— which he did often—attraction seemed to flare to life instantly.

Sunday he'd actually called his driver and had him take her to church. It was an interesting church, she thought, and then sighed, thinking it really hadn't been at all. It was nothing like she was used to. If that was the type of church Victor had grown up in, no wonder he was turned off by religion.

She vowed to ask around and find a different church for next Sunday.

Church was actually what had reminded her about the kids. That evening she'd called. She had wanted to make sure they were up and home from church first. The time difference was quite drastic from Holland to America. Holland was seven hours ahead of Louisiana.

She shouldn't have come. Mark and Susan were worried and upset and she found she hadn't slept much at all last night.

She couldn't toss and turn because the cast kept her anchored. At one point she'd awakened to find her other leg asleep because it was pinned under the cast.

She had black circles under her eyes, and she didn't feel like doing anything.

But Helga had shown up at her door this morning to help her dress.

So, she'd showered and slipped on the last of the four dresses she'd brought, a blue one that was straight and sleeveless. It tied around the waist.

Of course, it was too chilly outside to go anywhere in this dress, but then, she had found out the first day when trying to dress herself that she couldn't wear any of her pants because of the cast.

Helga did have a pair of hose for her this morning, however, saying she'd had Cook purchase them while in town. They were thigh-high hose, something she'd never worn, nor thought about wearing.

She was very grateful to Helga and thanked her—in Dutch no less. She managed to slip a stocking on the one leg that wasn't in the cast and then put a shoe on.

She felt much more together when she finally, slowly made her way down to breakfast.

Victor was waiting, reading the paper when she entered. He glanced up and his eyes lit up like Christmas lights. He immediately folded the newspaper and set it aside before standing.

"Goedemorgen," he said and repeated it in English, "Good morning."

"Goedemorgen," she repeated.

He smiled, the smile melting away the bad mood she'd awakened in. "You're getting better with your pronunciation."

"Thank you," she said, returning his smile.

"Dank u," he corrected.

"Dank u," she obediently repeated.

He reached her side and paused, lowering himself to her height to look into her eyes. "You had a bad night last night. You look tired."

Ah well, she had hoped he wouldn't notice with all of the makeup she'd applied. "I had trouble sleeping," she offered.

He took the crutches from her and rested them against a chair, then slipped an arm around her waist to help her to her seat.

So very physical, she thought and smiled in pleasure. She felt at home, strangely enough, with his touch.

"Is it the bed?" he asked.

She shook her head and eased down into the chair.

His hands slipped down, catching her left hand as he squatted next to her. "Are you in pain?"

He rubbed his thumb over the back of her hand gently, his eyes showing concern.

She couldn't let him go on thinking it was somehow his fault. "No. Actually, the crutches are causing me more pain than anything. But well…" she paused and glanced down at the plate in front of her.

"Yes?" he said, soft, low, the deep timbre of his voice inviting her to open up and share her burden.

"I called the kids last night."

She felt his hand tighten a bit before he said, "And this is what caused you not to sleep?"

She shrugged a bit. "They're very upset about me being here. They were really beside themselves when they found out I was staying in someone's chateau. They think you will kill me in the middle of the night for my money—or worse.'' She tried to chuckle but it didn't come out sounding much like a laugh.

Victor squeezed her hand and then stood. He paused behind her to rest both of his hands on her shoulders and press in a comforting gesture of warmth. ''But you're the mother and the wiser. You know you're safe. So why do you worry?''

''Because they're so upset.''

''Give them my phone number so they can contact you if they'd like,'' he offered.

Relief flooded through her. She'd felt funny asking for his phone number and was so glad he offered it. ''You don't mind?'' she questioned.

''You're a guest in my house. Of course I don't mind. If my son wanted to contact me, I'd want to make sure he had the phone number of where I was staying. Beyond that, however, Annie, you simply must allow your children to grow up and get along without you for eight weeks.''

He released her and strode back to his chair even as she gaped.

''Eight weeks? No, Victor. You misunderstood me the other day. I'm only planning to stay two weeks.''

He grinned that half grin of his and his eyes sparkled with amusement. ''You don't want to disappoint your friends who want you to stay eight weeks, do you?''

Annie rolled her eyes and then chuckled. ''You're impossible.''

He shook his head. ''No. I just like seeing you happy.''

''Why?'' she asked seriously.

His eyes turned dark and serious. ''Because you didn't get enough of it most of your life from what I've gathered, and,'' he said when she started to interrupt, ''when you're happy, it brings me joy.''

''Why?'' she asked again. ''You don't really know me.''

He shook his head. ''I'm not sure, Annie. But I do know that, inside me, a thirst is filled when I'm with you. Your laughter causes something to swell within me and even bubble over.''

His poetic words had her smiling. He had such a way of saying things sometimes.

''What is that smile for?'' he asked.

''I was thinking of your poem the other night that you read to me.''

''Ah, 'The Lament of an Empty Soul'?''

She nodded. ''It was very beautiful.''

He nodded once, bowing his head slightly and reminding her of a knight of old. ''I thank you.''

The maid showed up with breakfast and they ate. When they were done, Victor assisted Annie to a standing position. "How are you doing on the second floor?"

"If you didn't have the elevator, I'd be in trouble. But with that, it's manageable."

"The lift was put in to transport food from the basement to this floor, but whoever designed this house also made sure the upper floor was accessible as well. For breakfast in bed, I would guess."

"Well, I thank *you* for having it in the house."

"You're going to be chilly in that dress if we get out at any of the stops," he said as they started out of the dining room.

Annie sighed. "I know. But I only brought a few dresses and this is the last one I haven't worn."

"Don't you have any pants?" he asked, surprise in his voice.

She felt her cheeks heat. "Well, yes. But they don't fit over the cast."

He paused. "That would be a problem. Tell you what, why don't we get the housekeeper to alter them so they'll fit and then we'll see about finding you a sweater to wear today while we're out? When we return she can have at least one or two pairs of pants ready for you to wear."

"I don't want to put anyone out."

"You aren't. That's their job, Annie. They're servants. That's what they get paid to do."

She sighed. "I'm not used to servants."

He chuckled. "Trust me, they're used to doing things like this. Sometimes it's a lot more hectic. Just tell Helga what you'd like her to do and she'll see the message gets to the proper person."

He called for Helga and then quickly rattled off something in Dutch. When he was done, he turned to Annie and said, "The car is being brought around." He took the crutches from her and handed them to Helga and then scooped Annie up into his arms.

"I told you I'm too heavy for this."

He huffed as if out of breath and then said, "If—you're—too—heavy," *huff huff,* "I'll just… drop you," and acted as if he was about to drop her.

She gasped and latched on tightly.

He threw back his head and laughed. "Relax. How much do you weigh? One hundred and thirty? Forty? I lift weights and you're light compared to what I lift."

She flushed. "I'm not going to answer that question. Don't you know you should never ask a woman a question like that?" She weighed one hundred thirty-nine pounds and it was all in her hips as far as she was concerned.

He grinned cheekily. "You don't have to answer. I'll just go to the gym tomorrow and carry weights around until I figure it out.''

She growled in her throat, though there was no heat in it.

Victor chuckled again and bounced her slightly before heading out of the house. She couldn't believe how fast she'd adjusted to allowing Victor to help her around or carry her. It made her feel like a fairy princess in some ways, a Cinderella, living an entirely new life of discovery and surprise.

When they started down the stairs the car was waiting and the driver stood, holding the door open for them.

Victor allowed her feet to drop but kept his arms around her waist for a moment as he stared into her eyes. "My Cinderella," he murmured and a small smile played about his lips.

Oh brother, she should never have mentioned that to him. He was never going to let her live it down.

Looking into those eyes of his, she also realized she was getting herself into trouble here.

She hadn't misread him the other day. This was definitely something a stranger didn't do.

She felt an answering yearning inside herself. His arms holding her waist so closely to him, his gaze touching the planes of her face. She returned the stare, her gaze traveling lightly over his now-stubbled face, touching his lips, returning to his smoldering gaze.

Dangerous territory indeed.

She shuddered from the feelings that thrummed along her nerve endings.

Victor broke contact and cleared his throat, releasing her.

That fast, the electricity between them was gone, leaving her feeling short-circuited and as if she were missing out on the next step. She wasn't sure if she was upset or relieved. Still, she found she wanted to be around him. His poetry, their long talks, his sense of humor—they all drew her to him.

She turned and slid into the car, wondering if Victor even knew.

Boy did he know.

What had he been thinking?

He was attracted to this woman, but she wasn't the type of woman he dated.

She was what would be termed, in contemporary phrases, old-fashioned, a conservative chick or even worse expressions by some of the people he knew.

He didn't consider her any of those things, however. He thought she was a woman with a value system.

He'd almost kissed her.

But he wasn't looking for commitment right now, and if he started down that path, she was the type of woman who would expect it. He remembered too well the type of life he'd had with his parents. Their near hatred for others who weren't of 'the faith,' the rabid obsession that he keep all things worldly out of his life. He couldn't go back to that...and he wondered if Annie was like that at all. More and more he was realizing the Jesus his parents preached wasn't the same Jesus Annie was talking about. Still, it was there, deep down in him, that fear to commit and end up back in the bondage he'd once been in as a child. But what if Annie's description was real? What if it wasn't about a set of rules and regulations, but a relationship? What then?

He slid into the car and smiled politely at Annie, trying to see deeper into her, beyond what he knew. One thing he did know for sure, she'd mentioned her concern that her daughter was dating a man who wasn't a Christian.

She loved her kids and worried about them—too much in his opinion. And they manipulated her. Of course, who was he to talk about relationships?

Calling out instructions in Dutch to the driver on where to take them, he thought about Annie.

He didn't want to ruin what they had. He'd felt

so great around her, so happy for the first time in his life that he was certain a relationship would ruin it. That's what always happened. He just didn't know how to go about relationships—from his parents to his ex-wife to God. Relationships just never worked out.

Annie wasn't the type to enjoy life here for eight weeks and then leave…and honestly, he felt like a cad for even considering it.

Mentally drawing a line, he told himself she was to be off-limits. They would simply develop their friendship and that was it.

With that settled, he took a breath and let it out slowly, then turned to Annie. ''The windmill I'm taking you to see was built nearly one hundred and fifty years ago, if I remember its history correctly. It was constructed to help pump water. We're below sea level, and the people of the Netherlands had to come up with some ingenious ways to tame the land.''

''Are windmills very plentiful?'' she asked watching the countryside.

He followed her gaze to a small cottage surrounded by sheep and deep, tall, green grass. Life was so leisurely here, so laid-back compared to his hectic world. ''The windmills aren't as plentiful as they once were, though you can still find them around, much like the American lighthouses. They're there, but not used as they once were.''

The driver pulled up to a local shop which Victor sometimes frequented. ''I'll be right back,'' Victor said to Annie and was out of the car before she could comment.

Inside it took only a few minutes to find the soft cashmere sweater he wanted for her. It was light blue and very smooth. It would look beautiful on her. He paid for it and returned to the car.

''You'll need this.''

She gaped at the sweater he pulled out of the bag. ''You shouldn't have.''

''I wanted to.''

''I don't know of any lighthouses in Louisiana,'' Annie murmured, harkening back to their earlier conversation.

He leaned over and helped her slip on the delicate pastel sweater. Her skin was silky, and he again caught a whiff of that wonderful scent she wore.

The driver continued down the road. ''I think there might be one or two lighthouses,'' Victor replied.

She nodded absently, continuing to stare out at the beautiful, peaceful countryside. ''But…oh my…''

She'd spotted the windmill. Her earlier conversation was forgotten as her eyes took in the sight.

"It's big."

He nodded. "You can't quite get a feel of it if you don't see it in person."

"I get that feeling when I watch shows about the Pyramids of Giza."

"They're huge," he agreed.

"You've been there?" she asked, her gaze darting to his.

He nodded. "You need to go if you get the chance."

Her gaze was drawn back to the windmill. "Unfortunately, I'm not rich," she murmured, low enough that he didn't think she realized he'd heard.

Their worlds were so different, he thought. Those few words told it. She wasn't rich. She was starting a job in the fall because of that, and yet he could take off months, even years, if he wanted, because he had enough money to retire.

She wasn't used to servants. He never went without servants.

She talked about her three-bedroom house in a small, quiet neighborhood and his house was three floors with thirty-six rooms.

She thought he went to a gym. He had a gym in the basement.

But in other ways they were so alike. She loved

poetry, so did he. They both loved to paint and talk about horses and the list went on and on. Everything he mentioned, she was interested in, it seemed. Or she had an opinion on it.

The driver pulled up to a parking area and stopped.

Victor got out and came around to help Annie out.

"Wow," was all she said as she positioned the crutches and slowly swung her way toward the windmill.

"Look at the size of that thing. Look at the landscape around it. Aren't those wildflowers beautiful?"

It was like watching a child who'd been taken into a candy shop. Her gaze was everywhere, trying to take in everything and impressed by what she saw.

They walked around the windmill as well as going inside. When they came back out, he was grinning. "Not as impressive as you hoped?"

"I'm not sure what I expected," she replied. "I definitely wasn't impressed."

He wanted to impress her, he thought. "You like the flowers?" he asked waving his hand toward the field of wildflowers growing abundantly and unhindered.

She nodded. "I don't live out in the country

where there are wildflowers. And we certainly don't have these types in Louisiana."

He grinned. "Just a minute."

"What—" she started, but he ignored her.

Going off the path, he headed out into the field.

"Can you do that on private property? Will you get into trouble?" she called.

He laughed. "Laws are different here, Annie."

He bent down and started picking some of the white and pink wildflowers, gathering a beautiful bouquet for her.

"Oh dear!" She sounded distressed and excited both.

He glanced at her and waved. "Don't worry," he called out as he moved farther into the field to get some of the larger flowers. He glanced at her as he did, smiling broadly.

"Watch out!" she shouted.

"It's fine. Honest-t-agh!" He lost his footing on a rut or something.

Windmilling his hands, he tried to catch his balance and failed, falling headlong into a huge mud pit.

"Oh dear!"

He heard her shouted distress from where he lay, but, instead of being angry at his stupid maneuver, he began to laugh.

Pushing himself up, he noted he'd managed to

keep the flowers clean. If he'd sacrificed them, he probably would have missed most of the water in the puddle. Ah, what some people did trying to be gallant.

He stood and held up the bouquet.

She gasped as she took in the wet left side of him that was muddy and slimy, and then a giggle escaped.

And another.

By the time he got back to her, she was laughing as if she didn't have a care in the world.

"Your flowers, Annie Hooper," he said graciously and bowed slightly.

"Thank you, Mr. Rivers," she replied happily.

She gazed at the bouquet, the windmill forgotten, touching each tender petal with her long delicate fingers. "They're beautiful. I plan to take these home with me as a memory to cherish."

Her words warmed him right down to the depths of his empty, hurting soul. "I only need to think of how you look right now to have a memory of today."

Her gaze lifted to his and he saw the sparkle in her eyes before she glanced away. "We should get back home so you can change," she murmured.

He did his best to ignore what he'd seen in her eyes and simply nodded. "Yeah, I'm beginning to feel chilled. It's maybe fifteen degrees out today."

At her confused look, he added, "Celsius."

"That's right. Kilometers, Celsius. So many differences."

They both made their way back to the vehicle.

Once they were inside, the driver returned to the house. Victor realized it was almost lunchtime. They'd been gone longer than he'd thought.

"I'll go in and shower and ask Cook to prepare lunch. Sandwiches. If you'd like to dine in thirty minutes that'd be good for me."

She nodded. "I don't think I'll change. I want to keep the sweater on," she said, rubbing the soft arms and smiling. "This is absolutely beautiful."

Not as beautiful as you are, sitting there, he thought mildly.

"Then it sounds like a plan and…" he trailed off as he noticed the car pulling into his estate.

"It looks like you have company," Annie said brightly and a bit nervously, he thought.

He frowned.

He knew who it was.

Sean.

Sean, who knew more was going on with the woman at Victor's house than Victor had been letting on.

He was here to cause mischief.

"Victor?" Annie asked and he heard the worry.

He offered her a smile. ''Don't worry. It's a friend. You'll love him.''

Except that this friend was as famous as he was. He wondered if she would recognize him, if she would go ga-ga over him as so many other women did.

Sean was six-foot-two, tall, thin with short golden hair. Women tended to like that type, he thought.

He glanced sideways at the woman in the car with him.

''I can go upstairs if you'd like,'' she offered and he could tell she was nervous.

''No. It'll be fine. Just follow my lead.''

''Okay,'' she agreed, though he was sure she didn't understand. And neither did he. He had no idea where his sudden nervousness or possessiveness had come from, but he knew he didn't want Sean here right now when he was forming a friendship with this woman.

They drove up behind the other car. Sean was just getting out.

The driver halted Victor's car and opened the door.

Sean was standing, hands in pockets, looking totally relaxed, a smile on his face as he waited for Victor to exit the car.

Well, better now than waiting. He opened the door and slipped out. Sean started forward.

Victor turned and helped his guest from the car.

When he turned back to greet Sean he heard a gasp next to him and thought, *she's recognized him.*

"That's Sean Hampton. Isn't it?"

"Yes, it is."

"Oh my heavens! You didn't tell me you knew a movie star!"

Of course, Sean was close enough to hear that, and he cocked his head slightly. "Good morning," he said and nodded slightly to Annie, his eyes on Victor. "Are you going to introduce us?"

Victor turned to take the crutches from the driver and hand them to Annie who still clutched the bouquet in her hands.

She stood there, gaping like a besotted fan, at his friend, Sean, flowers forgotten. At Sean. She hadn't even recognized him. But she'd recognized Sean.

Victor couldn't stand it. He stepped in front of Annie and caught her attention.

She glanced at him, her eyes rounded in absolute shock as she accepted the crutches. "When I introduce you, Annie, say, *Ik ben van hem.*"

"What's that?" she whispered, casting a glance over his shoulder.

"It means welcome," he lied.

Turning back around, he nodded. "Hello, Sean. This is my guest, Annie Hooper. Annie, Sean Hampton."

Annie smiled shyly and then straightened her shoulders. *"Ik ben van hem,"* she said and smiled again.

Sean's right eyebrow went up and he cast a glance at Victor. "Ri-i-ight," he said.

Victor could tell Annie was confused by Sean's reaction and felt a bit guilty, but, he pushed the feeling aside, justifying it by the fact that Sean was a womanizer.

"Vertelde jij haar omdat te zeggen?" Sean asked in Dutch.

Of course I told her to say that, Victor thought but didn't answer. Instead, he smiled and slipped his arm around Annie's shoulders, being careful not to get her wet. "We've been out touring the local windmills."

"You look as though you've been visiting with the local swine, old boy," Sean said crisply.

"Maybe you should go in and change, Victor," Annie suggested.

"Victor?" Sean asked, his eyebrow going back up.

Annie glanced from one to the other. "I should

leave you with your special guest,'' she said nervously.

"Special guest?'' Sean repeated in a query.

It was going to come out. Victor wasn't going to be able to stop it. "She means you, Sean. She recognized you as a movie star.''

Sean's smile turned slightly cynical before he shook his head in confusion. Chuckling, he asked, "But how does that make me special, Jake, since you…''

"She doesn't know.''

"I say,'' Sean replied. "How can that be?''

"Jake?'' Annie asked. "Jake…'' Annie's confusion was obvious as she glanced from Sean to Victor and back again. Then her eyes widened as recognition dawned. "Oh my heavens. Jake as in *Jake* Rivers!''

"It seems she knows now,'' Sean said simply.

Victor glared at Sean. "I'll meet you inside.''

"Good thing,'' Sean said. "I could use some lunch.''

He headed up the long set of stairs.

"Tell Cook to have it ready in thirty minutes.''

Victor returned his attention to his guest and the questions she was going to have.

Chapter Seven

"**Y**ou're Jake Rivers, the actor," Annie accused Victor before Sean was completely out of sight.

She hadn't meant to sound angry, but she was absolutely floored, embarrassed, upset…she wasn't sure what she was. "Why did you tell me you were Victor?"

"That's my name. The name I act under is Jake Rivers."

She opened her mouth to reply and paused. That made sense. But why did she feel so betrayed?

"I thought you'd recognize me at the hospital." He shrugged. "Most people do. It was quite a blow to my ego when you didn't, even more so when you recognized Sean just now."

She felt her cheeks heating up in embarrassment. "You could have told me."

"And have you looking at me the way you just did at Sean?" Victor asked and then shook his head. "You enchant me, Annie. You are such a lovely person, such a gentle person. I enjoy your company. Sean was supposed to come up the day after the wreck to rest for a few weeks before the premiere of a new movie we're in together, but I put him off. He evidently decided to come up anyway."

She stared at him suspiciously.

He returned her stare, his features inscrutable.

"You're an actor. How do I know if you're lying to me?"

"Annie, that's not fair," he said simply.

She rubbed her forehead. "Oh dear," she muttered. "I can't believe this. That's why all of those photographers were at the hospital," she suddenly said and gasped as she realized that was why he'd kept looking so oddly at her that day. He'd expected her to recognize him.

He held out his hands. "Just calm down."

She swatted at them, and then realized she must be really upset to do that. "Don't treat me like a child."

He lifted his hands up on either side. "I wasn't trying to do that, Annie. Look, Annie, I'm sorry. I should have simply been honest with you, but how could I do that without sounding egotistical?"

She thought about that.

"I guess you couldn't have."

"And we were having such a good time."

She had to agree with that.

"Can't we just go back to how things were?"

She paused and studied him. "You looked familiar to me when I first saw you."

"Well that's a relief," he said and smiled.

She found herself smiling back. "It's the hair and beard. You don't wear it like that in publicity photos."

He shrugged. "The last movie I did called for long hair. So, after the movie was over, I decided to keep it. It has some natural curl and women seem to like it." He grinned very egotistically this time.

She swatted at him again. "I can't compete with the crowd you run with. I don't know that I want to. What am I even doing here?"

Okay, she sounded silly, but all of these insecurities were making themselves known. Jake Rivers was one of the biggest actors in America since his last film. No one knew a lot about him except that he was a fine actor and *Storm Clouds* had catapulted him into mega-famous status from simply famous. The movie had been nominated for thirteen Academy Awards.

Victor reached up and grabbed her by the shoulders, forcing her with his mere presence to look at him. What she saw there was an earnest look of honesty and entreaty. "You don't have to compete with anyone, Annie. Don't you realize that's why I enjoy your company? You're different. You are solid and you bring me joy, a joy I haven't felt in a very long time."

Annie started to protest but a small check in her spirit reminded her of what she had thought to herself only a short time ago. This man was lonely.

Knowing now who he was, she would have said there was no way that he was lonely. But having gotten to know the man before she knew the reputation, she had to admit he was not what the press made him out to be. At least not with her.

Of course, he was an actor; he could be lying to her, playing out some strange staged events to get what he wanted.

But she wasn't important enough for him to do that, so she shrugged it off.

"Annie?" he asked softly, rubbing her shoulders in a gentle, soothing motion.

She nodded. "We can try to go on. But are you sure you want me here around your real friends?"

He blinked. "I don't believe you just said that."

"Said what?" He looked offended and upset.

"I thought we were developing a friendship," he said simply.

''We are.'' She admitted her statement had been stupid, but chalked it up to the fact she was still reeling from her fresh discoveries.

He nodded. ''Then you're one of my friends too. Now, can we go inside before I freeze?''

She glanced down and remembered he was wet. ''Oh dear. I can let myself in. You go on.''

He shook his head. ''You can't go up all of those stairs in that cast.''

He glanced toward the front door and then sighed. ''I don't want to get you wet.''

He hesitated and then met her gaze again. ''Wait right here.''

He headed up the stairs, and in a minute Sean came sauntering out.

''I've been asked to assist you,'' he said simply.

She swallowed. ''Oh, I don't know. I mean—''

Sean didn't allow her to argue but took the crutches and handed them to Helga, who followed quietly behind him. He then leaned down and lifted her into his arms. ''I am to tell you that Jake— Victor,'' he corrected, ''went upstairs to change. He'll join us as soon as he is done.''

Annie felt light-headed. Here was this handsome movie star carrying her and she'd just found out Victor was Jake Rivers.

''Nice flowers,'' he murmured and she realized they were right under his chin.

"You're not allergic are you? Victor picked them for me."

Sean shook his head. *"Victor,"* he murmured and smiled. "So you really didn't know who Jake was?" he asked bemusedly.

She frowned at his amused tone. "He's a nice man."

"Nice?" Sean repeated, a grin spreading across his handsome features.

"Yes. He's very nice and gentlemanly."

"Gentleman—"

"—ly. Yes," she repeated and her voice contained a note of warning.

It did no good. Sean burst into laughter.

They reached the top of the stairs, and he allowed her body to slide down his body—nice and slow and very forward. "Gentlemanly, is it?" he asked and she was aghast at how easily he turned on the charm.

Good heavens, it oozed from every pore of his body and all of it was aimed at her. His gaze could have started a forest fire with the spark of heat it contained. His hands slid up her waist to her back as if he were steadying her. And more...his body language...

She stepped on his toe with her cast.

He gasped and immediately released her.

That turned off the charm all right.

"Oh, I'm sorry," she said, feigning surprise. She clutched the flowers to her chest. "I didn't see your foot there."

He glared at her.

She gratefully accepted the crutches from the gaping Helga. She handed the flowers to her. "Please put these in water in my room."

Helga nodded.

Annie quickly positioned the crutches and said, "Shall we wait in the parlor? Maybe I should send Helga for some ice for that injury?"

"That act could earn you an Academy Award, sweetheart," Sean muttered darkly. "I think I'll pass on the ice." He straightened.

She turned and started swinging herself into the parlor.

Once inside the parlor, Annie found a chair to sit in, just to make sure she had plenty of room away from Mr. Charming, though she didn't think he was a prince, but a frog for his attempt to charm her right in his own friend's house.

He obviously recognized her tactic because he sent her another one of those amused grins and walked across the room to look out the window.

"You have wants of anything?" Helena asked in severely accented English as she came into the room to check on them.

A fireplace poker, Annie thought but said instead, "Some water please." She wondered if the woman even understood her. By the look on her face, she doubted she did. She started to shake her head no, but Sean spoke to her in Dutch.

Helena replied and left the room.

Annie really wished she spoke Dutch. What had he said to Helena?

"It's lovely this time of year here in Holland," Sean said, casually.

"I'll take your word for it," Annie replied.

"Where are you from?" he continued, not turning from his place by the window.

Annie relaxed. "Louisiana."

"American," Sean said.

"Born and raised there. This is my first time out of the state."

He turned, both eyebrows raised. "You don't say? In today's world I find that quite unusual."

She smiled politely. "My family lived there. I had no reason to leave."

"No husband to drag you off on vacations? No kids?"

She knew he was teasing, so she shocked him by replying, "My husband has been dead four years. My son is over thirty and my daughter just a year younger."

Oh yeah, she'd shocked him. She could see him

adding it up. "So, that makes you older than Jake."

She grinned and shook her head. "Not at all."

"I see."

"I'm sure you do. With my husband dead, I'm looking for a fortune to help raise my kids."

He actually gaped.

Her smile widened.

And then he laughed. "Definitely Academy Award material, Annie. You're too young to have children that old and you told me yourself you didn't know who Jake was."

"As you wish," she said simply.

The housekeeper, Helena, returned with a tray. On it she had two glasses of clear liquid. She guessed it was either wine or something she didn't recognize, as she doubted Mr. Hampton was drinking water too. Then again—after meeting Victor she was learning not to make assumptions.

"*Dank u,*" she said politely to the maid.

"You speak Dutch?" Sean said, surprised.

She smiled. "Yes," she replied and added silently, a few words, thanks to Victor aka Jake.

"Sorry I took so long," Victor said, coming into the room.

Annie's expression brightened; she felt much easier now that Victor was there.

Victor came over and stopped by her chair. Reaching out he took her hand and squeezed it. "Problems getting inside?" he asked.

She lifted an eyebrow. He knew somehow, she thought. "Not at all," she replied.

He frowned slightly, then turned. Walking over to his friend he held out his hand and shook hands. "I told you next week, bud," Victor said lightly.

"I could not contain my curiosity," Sean replied easily.

"I figured as much. I should kick you out right on your—"

"But you won't," Sean interrupted. "You know I'd win."

"Oh yeah?" Victor replied.

Male bonding, Annie thought wearily. Men!

"If you'll excuse me," Annie said, and pushed herself up to stand.

Both men turned.

She smiled. "I'm going into lunch before you two start throwing punches to prove your masculinity."

"Oh, mine isn't in question, sweetheart," Sean replied immediately.

"Neither is his," Annie muttered under her breath.

"What was that?" Sean asked.

"She said she had grave doubts," Victor filled in. He was already by her side and had slipped an arm around her waist. With his other hand he scooped up the crutches. "Come on," he called back to Sean.

Embarrassed, Annie refused to look at Sean. She could use the crutches and didn't need Victor to lean on. But then, this felt good as well. She slipped her arm around him.

"Did you know she has a son that is over thirty," Sean continued, grinning. "And that she is after your fortune?"

Victor came to her rescue. "She does have a son over thirty and a daughter too. And if she is here after my fortune," he turned a warm gaze down on her and said gently, "I'm sure she'll confess that to me soon."

Sean paused behind his seat in the dining room. "You do not have a son who is over thirty. Tell me this man is not dating an older woman?"

She broke off her gaze from Victor and smiled at Sean. "I do have a son that is over thirty. And Victor is not dating an older woman."

"But…"

Victor grinned. "He is her stepson."

"Spoilsport," Annie said low, her gaze fully on Victor.

Victor eased Annie into her chair and then propped her crutches next to her. "Young one," he said grinning.

"I certainly feel it at the moment," she replied blushing at his blatant flirtation.

Sean cleared his throat. "So, sandwiches is all you can afford?" he asked, looking at what was brought in. "Should I be worried that you're not getting good contracts like me?"

"I told her sandwiches were fine since Annie didn't mind and I wasn't expecting company."

"Touchè, old boy," Sean replied.

Annie bowed her head for a quick prayer. When she lifted her gaze, Sean was staring at her with the strangest look on his face.

"So, how are your injuries from the last movie you just finished up?" Sean asked and then drew his gaze away from Annie. He wasn't grinning anymore but studying his friend thoughtfully.

Annie had lifted her sandwich to eat, intending simply to listen and not participate in the conversation. She wasn't quite ready to be in the company of two of the biggest stars in show business. But when she heard him mention Victor was injured she blurted out, "You were hurt?"

He nodded. "I was on set when a board fell. It caught me in the side and bruised it up pretty good.'' He glanced back to his friend. ''It's fine, barely yellow now.''

''Did you rehurt it in the wreck?'' Annie asked worriedly.

Victor shot his friend a glare. ''No, Annie. I'm fine.''

''No residual damage from the wreck?'' Sean asked, taking a bite of his sandwich roll. He chewed it with gusto as he awaited his friend's answer.

''Nope. Not even sore today, though Annie can't say the same thing.'' He glanced over at her. ''At the appointment later today we'll see about a walking cast. Those crutches have you moving slowly and stiffly.''

''I can't believe how much pain crutches can cause,'' she agreed. ''They're supposed to help a person, not hinder them.''

''Is the pain medication helping?''

She glanced at Sean, saw him watching her and then glanced back. ''Yes. Thank you, again, Victor, for all of your help.''

''Annie,'' Victor said and she heard the warning in his voice. He hated her to keep thanking him when he felt it was his fault. She shrugged.

''Dank u?'' she said cheekily.

He broke into laughter and shook his head.

''You know very well what I meant.'' He turned

to Sean and smiled. "Sean is here because our new movie will be premiering in two weeks."

"Really? Oh!" Annie's eyes widened. "*Shadow*…no *Shelter,* right?

"I remember hearing about it, but I didn't remember you being…er…" She saw Sean grin at the fact that she would have recognized him in it but not Victor. She glared at him. "That's right, you play the hero, don't you?" she asked Victor, pointedly turning her attention to him.

Sean's smile disappeared. "We're both heroes."

"Oh?"

Victor looked from one to the other and chuckled. "Sheath the claws, Annie. Stop baiting Annie, Sean. I play a knight in a fantasy. He is looking for an ancient shelter that contains the protection the world needs to survive. Sean is my sidekick who is there to keep me on the straight and narrow."

"I wasn't sure from the trailer exactly what it was about," she replied.

"Yeah, the trailer wasn't that well put together," Sean muttered, turning his attention to Victor. "I wonder how that is going to affect box-office stats."

"You know with you in it we'll have every woman under thirty knocking down the doors at the theater," Victor replied simply.

"Funny, old man," Sean said.

Evidently this was an ongoing thing between the two, Annie thought, as she watched the banter between them. "I like mine older, thank you very much. You're the one who likes them young," Sean said.

Victor cast a glance at Annie and cleared his throat.

"And how old are you?" Sean asked, smiling at Annie.

"Forty," she replied simply.

"Poaching on my territory, I say," Sean said to Victor.

He shot a look at his friend. "So, who are you taking to the premiere?" he asked, changing the subject.

Sean shrugged and took another bite of his sandwich. "I thought about Helena, but she wouldn't have me," he said referring to the housekeeper and being totally outrageous. "So, I'll settle with Reanna. She's been wanting to go to a premiere for a while and I think she'll enjoy this one."

"And you?" Sean asked and then winced as if he'd said something wrong. He glanced guiltily at Annie.

Annie wasn't sure what was meant by that until Victor said, "I was planning on taking no one, just calling Meredith who played one of the lead parts,'' he said in an aside to Annie, ''and seeing if she'd go. But,'' and his gaze turned fully to Annie. ''If Annie will do me the honor, I'll take her to the premiere.''

Annie nearly choked on the mouthful of sandwich she was chewing.

Chapter Eight

"Are you all right?" Victor started to stand.

Annie held up her hand and wheezed, attempting to swallow what was in her mouth.

Even Sean looked concerned. "Jake?" he said.

Annie shook her head and swallowed. She grabbed her water glass and drained it, and then promptly spewed water as she coughed and gasped again.

"Jake," Sean said really alarmed.

"Annie?" Victor stood and started toward her.

"You—you can't be—serious."

Seeing she was talking, albeit a bit raspily, Victor reluctantly took his seat.

She picked up her napkin and dabbed at her mouth and then the table.

Sean picked up his own napkin and began to dab at himself.

"I am quite serious," Victor replied, the only one not dabbing.

"Oh dear," she whispered.

"Annie?" Victor asked gently.

When she didn't look up, Victor reached over and took her hand into his. "Is there a problem?"

She glanced up quickly at him and then back down.

Sean cleared his throat, uncomfortable.

"I'm not…well…I'm just plain Annie, Victor. I've seen the premieres on TV. You're not supposed to appear with someone like me."

Victor squeezed her hand. "I thought we were friends," he said again and Annie sighed.

"Well, yes."

"Look at me, Annie."

She glanced nervously at Sean, who was sipping his water and then her gaze lifted to Victor's. "I want to take you. I had planned on waiting a day or two more to ask, but then Sean showed up."

Reminded of Sean's presence, Annie's gaze darted that way and then back. She wasn't used to having an audience.

Victor felt her hands, slick with perspiration, and realized how nervous she was. Gently, he began drawing circles on the back of her hand with his thumb, totally ignoring his friend. "It'd be an experience you could take back and tell your friends," he said, tenderly, smiling, turning on the charm.

She weakened some. He saw it in her eyes and the way her shoulders relaxed a bit. If Sean would not say anything, he could probably convince her.

"But I don't have clothes like that to wear. You've seen all the dresses I have with me," she admitted desperately.

Victor blinked. "Is that all?" His smile invited her to smile with him. "We'll find something. Clothes are the least of our worries. My biggest worry is being there without a date and having to face the leading lady, Meredith."

She was wavering. She chewed her lip and wrinkled her nose up in indecision.

"Please, Annie. It'll be fun, and it would be an honor for me to have someone who can actually carry on a conversation, especially someone that makes me laugh like you do."

"I wouldn't know what to do."

"You would have to do nothing except grace my arm with your presence."

He paused and saw her wilting. "It's a once-in-a-lifetime thing. You'll love it. It's even better than windmills and wildflowers."

She was defeated. Her shoulders slumped and

she laughed. "Even better than that?" she asked. "Well how can I resist?"

"I promise it won't interfere with our tour of Holland." He squeezed her hand.

She glanced over and was reminded of Sean's presence. A dull flush climbed up her cheeks. Glancing down at her dress, she winced. "I need to change before the doctor's appointment."

Victor stood and moved behind Annie. He slipped a hand under her arm and assisted her to a standing position. She wasn't far from him and he took the moment to inhale her sweet scent again. "Thank you again," he said softly.

She glanced up and their gazes connected. He saw something there, he wasn't sure what, and then it was gone. "I'll be back down in time for the appointment."

He reluctantly released her arm and allowed her to go her own way.

When she was gone, he continued to stare after her.

"Just friends?" Sean asked, disbelief rife in his voice.

Victor turned to Sean. "Yes. We're friends."

Sean blew out air, pursing his lips as he did. "Please, dear boy. How long have I known you?"

Victor waved him off and took his seat.

Sean changed tactics. "She's not your size-three starlet or the model you usually date."

"I'll agree to that," Victor said. He took the last bite of his sandwich.

"A bit clumsy if you ask me," Sean added.

Victor stared at his friend. "She just found out who I am and met you. I think a lesser person would have really made a scene. Personally, I think she took the news well—especially since I had no time to prepare her for the invitation."

"Ah, the invitation." Sean nodded. "Are you sure about that? You know the media is going to eat her alive. Just what do you know about her? I mean, her reputation and all. It wouldn't do to be seen with a former...uh...nah, never mind," Sean said.

"Yeah. She's not a former anything. She's a very nice widow from Louisiana."

"What are you going to do about her clothes?" he asked.

Victor shrugged. "Call a designer and have her send a couple of dresses here."

Sean nodded. "I'll do my best to help deflect questions and such, but you know how the media is."

"Yeah," Victor said and sighed.

"Are you sure you know what you're doing here, Jake? I do say, if you're just friends, you could break it off now and possibly avoid any disasters.''

"I want her to go with me," Victor replied.

Sean paused, studying his friend intently as he sipped his water. Finally he said, "You made her say, 'I'm his,' when I arrived today."

"It was a joke," Victor replied. It hadn't been at the time. He'd actually been jealous of his friend. But he wasn't going to admit that to him. He'd never been jealous of Sean—not like this. Maybe because of the look on Annie's face when she'd recognized Sean. All he knew for certain was that he hadn't liked the feeling in him when she had looked at Sean.

Sean nodded. "I hope so, otherwise you might just be serious about this woman. And personally I find her fascinating."

He knew what Sean was fishing for—a reaction. Instead of satisfying Sean, he picked up his glass and took a sip of wine. "She's already taken. I'm escorting her to the premiere, remember?"

He nodded. "That you are. But that doesn't mean she can't be interested in someone else, does it?"

If he said yes, then Sean would have proven a point. If he said no, then Sean would set about to prove a point.

Luckily, he was saved by the ringing of the

phone. "I'm expecting a call. Excuse me," he said and stood.

"I'll take my regular room. I'm exhausted and need a nap. See you later this afternoon?" Sean asked, standing.

Victor nodded and headed out of the dining room, thinking he wasn't sure he was ready to face Sean and his usual pranks.

Annie heard the phone but didn't think anything about it until Helena showed up and said in broken English, "Telephone."

She nodded and picked up the extension next to her bed. "Hello?"

She was surprised to hear the lodge on the phone, calling to see if she wanted them to continue to hold her reservations. She was glad to know the man on the other end spoke broken English. She thought about it and then answered, "No. Thank you, but I'll not need them at least for three more days. Can you cancel up through then?"

She was assured it was no problem before disconnecting. Five days. If she only stayed two weeks, then she would be leaving in a week. But she'd agreed to go to a premiere in less than two weeks, so she'd be staying at least three weeks...

She replaced the receiver and stood before the mirror to look at her outfit.

She had on a pair of blue jeans with a tiny braided belt and she'd put on the blue sweater. Instead of a secondary piece of clothing, she'd buttoned it up as a primary top. It looked great that way. They might not wear them like this in Holland, but they did in America. She'd seen others wearing tops like this and she liked the sweater so much that she decided to go for it.

Her pants were let out one-quarter of the way up—just enough room for them to slip over her cast—and then hemmed up the side. They looked great.

She wished she knew who to thank for the alterations.

She quickly combed her hair and then checked her makeup. She started to put her hair back up but paused.

It looked so stark that way. That was how she usually wore it since it was so long, but perhaps…

She thought about braiding it and then shook her head. She pulled it back into a ponytail but thought, too young.

With a sigh she gave up and walked out of the room—and nearly ran down Victor.

Catching her by the arms, he steadied her. "Why are you looking so glum?" he asked curiously. He had his coat in his hand and was headed toward the stairs. He released her and turned, slipping an arm behind her back as he did.

"Your hair!"

He grinned and ran a hand over his short hair. "Did I mention a barber was coming to cut my hair today?"

"No."

He chuckled.

"You shaved your beard too," she said noting how clean-shaven he was.

He nodded. "Back to the normal look."

She thought if he'd looked like that when she first saw him, there would have been no mistaking him for who he was. Wow, he was drop-dead gorgeous.

Together they started toward the elevator. "It's silly but I didn't feel like putting my hair up and so I left it down, but it just looks so plain."

"So change it."

She glanced up at him. "What?"

He grinned. "Change it."

He opened the lift and allowed her to go in first.

"Haven't you ever thought about it?" he asked.

"Well, yes," she admitted. "But...I just don't know how I'd do it."

"There's a place in town I go to occasionally. As a matter of fact, the stylist that cut my hair today is from there. Let's go by. Pick out something you want and have them design a new style. Yvonne will be able to advise you. She has exquisite taste.''

''You're serious?'' she asked and reached up to touch her hair.

He touched his own hair reminding her of *his* new look. ''Yes. I'm serious.'' He mocked her and she found herself laughing in return.

''When I got tired of this, all I had to do was cut it. Same with you. Or you can add highlights or a dozen other things.''

She thought about it and then thought how much she was saving by not being at the lodge. She had enough money to do something with her hair. ''Why not?'' she said and grinned.

''That's the spirit,'' Victor said and shot a fist up in the air.

She laughed. ''To spirit.''

''Yeah,'' he growled.

She shook her head, wondering what this man was doing to her. She'd only just left the dining room a short time before, her emotions in an uproar over going to a theatrical premiere. She'd made a mess of the table, spat water all over Sean Hampton and was so jittery she hadn't been sure she would make it to her room before she collapsed.

But back alone with Victor he was able to calm her and change her glumness and worry into fun and laughter.

How did he do it?

She wasn't sure how, but she did know she was certainly glad she had met him.

Chapter Nine

"I can't buy this," Annie said and laughed.

She held up an outrageous blouse that was so very European.

"It'd look great on you, especially with that new hairstyle," Victor said.

She smiled up into his eyes. "You really like it?"

He reached up and cupped the back of her head. "I love it." Gently, he massaged her head.

Someone cleared their throat.

They both turned toward the cashier. "Buy it, and I'll take you horseback riding, after a fashion, later this afternoon," he said.

She laughed. "Okay. But I'm holding you to that."

She pulled out her money and allowed Victor to help her count out how much she owed.

He took the bag and then slipped his hand behind her back as they started out of the store.

They'd been gone from the house for three hours now. Her haircut had taken nearly an hour and then they'd gone to the doctor. Finally Victor had insisted on taking her to some of the tourist shops. They had just happened to stop in this tiny boutique as an afterthought.

"How are you faring?" Victor asked now as they headed toward the car.

"I can't tell you how much fun I've had," she said, feeling happy through and through.

"Me too."

He opened the door and tossed the bag into the back seat. "Annie—" he started.

She glanced up, smiling. "Yes?"

A person riding by on a bike rang his bell and the mood was broken. "Nothing," he replied.

He took the crutches and slipped them into the back seat.

"There sure are a lot of bicycles here," she said seeing another pass by.

He nodded. "Everyone rides bicycles. I have some at home."

She sighed. "I haven't been on one in forever. I don't know if I can still ride."

"Well you aren't going to be on one soon, either," he said and looked pointedly at her cast. He opened the front passenger door for her and she lowered herself into the seat.

"Next week, the doctor said. A walking cast next week."

He grinned. "I imagine not being able to bend your knee is truly a challenge."

She nodded. "The doctor really is a nice man."

Victor agreed.

He closed her door and went around to the driver's side. Sliding in, he pulled it closed behind him, locking out the outside world.

"You have a well-insulated car," she said, quietly, feeling the tension between them.

"Annie," he turned toward her. He reached up and ran his fingers through her hair.

Her smile faded and her gaze focused on him. "Yes?"

He leaned forward and instead of kissing her, he rested his cheek against her cheek. She heard him inhale. Her entire body reacted to that simple gesture.

He whispered, "You've changed my life since you've been here. I wanted you to know that."

She wasn't sure what he meant or why he sounded the way he did.

The soft raspy whisper against her ear had her

wanting more than talk. She turned her head only slightly, allowing her lips to brush just below his ear.

She heard his swift intake of breath.

A car horn sounded.

He pulled back.

Oh dear. Had she misread him? she wondered.

He turned his attention forward and started the car. "I just wanted to mention…"

He glanced around and pulled out into traffic. "Sean is a friend, but he likes to…well…"

"Yes?" she asked when he didn't continue.

"Sean is Sean. We're like brothers. He's the best friend I have, actually. And he watches out for me. He's a bit protective of me."

She chuckled. "Protective?"

He chuckled as well. "It's a long story. I wasn't the happiest person when I started acting and I was very wild. Sean took it upon himself to rein me in somewhat and help guide my career. He helped me find a good agent and got me into some bit parts in his movies. That's why we've been in so many movies together. Our on-screen meetings continued occasionally until this year. He found a great fantasy movie series and contacted me, telling me to read for it. We both got parts. We've done two of a three-part movie series already this year with the third one scheduled for next year. What I'm trying to say is that I hope you can be patient with him.''

She wasn't sure *what* he was saying, but he was dancing around something. ''You know I will. I'm a guest in your house. I wouldn't offend someone else.''

She thought about asking him about Sean's actions earlier, but then decided that it wasn't important. It sounded as if he and Sean were very close.

Perhaps Sean hadn't meant anything by his actions. She felt out of her league with these men anyway now that she realized just how experienced they were in the world.

Back at the house Victor slipped out of the car and came around to lift Annie into his arms.

He had tried to explain that Sean was suspicious about her. He'd seen it in the way Sean studied Annie. Victor wasn't as cynical as Sean. Sean didn't believe Annie really hadn't known who he was. And Sean was out to force Victor to recognize something that he wasn't ready to admit to. Didn't think he could admit. Wouldn't admit.

''Ready?'' he asked and scooped her up.

She chuckled. ''Yes,'' she said after the fact.

He laughed as well and started up the stairs.

Sean worried about him. He knew about the bad relationship he'd had with his parents and that he'd not really gotten over it. Sean was certain that was why none of his relationships worked out. And maybe he was right.

Today in town had been wonderful however. Victor loved just holding Annie's hand. He'd always been a physical person, even with his son, so he wasn't surprised he liked to touch Annie.

But he'd almost kissed her in the car.

He'd realized he wanted that more than anything, and it had really shocked him because he was afraid he was feeling much more than simple friendship now—and he didn't know when exactly that had happened.

Victor topped the stairs with his bundle, nodding back toward the car where he'd left the crutches when Helga came out.

It had taken every ounce of strength he had not to act on his impulse. When he'd felt her lips brush his cheek near his ear he had nearly come unglued.

He'd decided getting Annie home where he wasn't alone with her was his best bet if he was going to keep from acting on his physical impulses.

He reminded himself again that relationships did not work out where he was concerned.

Sean knew how to push his buttons.

Had he not realized Sean had done something to Annie this morning when he'd carried her in, he probably wouldn't have been so obsessed with kissing Annie.

He wasn't sure what had happened, but he was certain Sean had said or done something to find out if what she'd said about not knowing Victor was true. Perhaps he was trying to find any hidden motives.

His friend could be ruthless sometimes. And now Victor's mind was obsessing with Annie because of it.

Entering the house, he glanced down at Annie. "Should I put you down now or carry you into the library?"

"You have a library?"

He smiled. "Helga didn't show you?"

"We saw the back half of the house."

Helga showed up with the crutches.

Victor released her, allowing her feet to drop to the floor. He stepped back, reluctantly.

"*Dank u*, Helga," Annie said graciously and accepted the crutches.

The maid nodded and hurried off.

"Well, well, well," Sean said. He was just coming down the stairs. "What have we here?"

His eyes were on Annie.

"Hello, Sean," Victor replied.

Sean finished coming down the stairs and walked up to Annie. "I say." He reached up and ran his fingers into her hair. "This is absolutely stunning, sweetheart."

Her eyes widened in surprise at his actions.

She glanced to Victor, who simply stood staring, his face a blank mask.

She pulled back simply by turning on her crutches to go toward the room Victor had indicated was the library. "Thank you. I like it too, Mr. Hampton."

"Sean, sweetheart. Call me Sean."

She didn't look back or reply. Victor hadn't said a word, and she was certain she saw something more than appreciation in Sean's eyes.

Maybe Sean was just a very forward man, meaning nothing by it. Victor after all, was very physical. Actors had to be, she supposed, though she didn't want Sean being too physical with her. Now Victor, on the other hand...

She paused. "I have to call my children and let them know I'm staying longer," she said.

"You go on into the library. We'll join you there shortly," Victor said.

She nodded. *"Dank u,"* she replied.

Victor waited until the door closed before turning to his friend. "What was that all about?"

Sean blinked in surprise. "What was what all about?" he asked innocently.

"The charm you just turned on."

"Are you interested?" Sean asked. His gaze pierced Victor.

Victor gave his friend a pointed look. "Of course not. As I told you earlier, she's just a friend."

"Then you don't mind if I—?"

"She's also quite innocent, Sean."

"Please," Sean rebuked. "She was married for several years. I wouldn't call her innocent."

"I'm not talking about sex, Sean," Victor replied. "I'm talking about her spirit. She's not jaded and hardened the way we are."

"So, you care for her?" Sean asked.

Victor studied his friend. "As a friend."

Something flashed in Sean's eyes and then he shrugged. "As you wish. You won't mind if I pursue her then?"

"Be my guest. Just don't hurt her."

What else could he say? Maybe it was for the best. He refused to deepen the relationship with her. He'd simply make sure Sean wasn't alone with her while he was here. How hard could that be?

"If you'll excuse me, I promised Annie we'd go riding when we got home."

"In a cast?" Sean asked, surprised.

Victor smiled. "We'll manage. I have a few plans up my sleeve."

Chapter Ten

Annie was so excited.

Victor was going to church with her.

At first he wasn't going to go. But as they'd sat around after dinner last night, Annie had mentioned to Victor that Helga had told her that her sister had a friend who attended another church and Annie would like to go to it.

Victor had offered her his driver again. And Annie was about to settle for that when Sean had offered to go with her.

Alarmed, she'd glanced at him. She didn't want to be alone with him in a car—but she certainly wouldn't tell him not to attend church.

Sean's offer had gotten Victor's attention, which actually cheered Annie. He'd suddenly asked what type of church it was. Annie had explained it was very different from the first one she'd attended.

Nodding, he'd said very casually that he thought he would attend with her.

Sean had smiled smugly—at what she wasn't sure—those two had secrets constantly going on between them—and then he'd said he'd be ready in the morning.

Victor had helped her upstairs afterward.

And now here it was, the next morning, and Annie was heading down the elevator, barely able to contain herself.

She couldn't believe Victor was going to church with her.

She'd known he'd been watching her for several days now, and often when it was only she and Victor in the room, he would sometimes question her about her life as a Christian.

He shrugged it off, but she thought it had something to do with his past.

Coming into the foyer she found both Sean and Victor waiting.

Sean smiled politely and Victor came forward. "You're looking beautiful this morning," he said and took her hand.

He didn't look really happy about going, but he did seem to be appreciative that she was wearing the sweater he'd bought her.

"Thank you."

"Ravishing," Sean said.

She nodded politely.

Victor escorted her to the car and assisted her into the back seat, sliding in after her.

Sean went around and climbed in on the opposite side.

Great. She was stuck in between them.

"So, Sean, is this your first time in church?"

Victor snorted.

Sean lifted a brow. "Do you think I am that uncouth, my dear?"

She flushed.

Victor snorted. "Give it a rest, Sean. Answer Annie."

Sean smiled at his friend. "Actually, I've attended a few times here and there. All kinds of...spiritual ceremonies."

"Spiritual..."

"...ceremonies. In other words, friends getting married or..."

"I think she gets the idea, Jake," Sean said.

"Ah." Indeed she did.

"Well they will probably greet us, then sing and have a time for sharing a message and then prayer. Pretty simple."

Sean chuckled. "If this turns out that simple..." He trailed off. She glanced up at him and then to Victor and wondered why both looked so cynical.

However, she didn't ask, and eventually they arrived at the small church. "Helga said it runs about a hundred people."

"This is a church?" Sean asked.

"Bigger than the one my parents had," Victor murmured.

It was a small square brick building out on the edge of town. Cars were parked in the gravel and grass around it. A tall man in a suit and tie stood at the front door chatting with someone else. They glanced curiously at the car when it pulled up.

"Well here goes," Victor said.

Annie wasn't sure what he meant.

But she was disturbed when his demeanor changed, and both he and Sean suddenly wore plastic smiles.

Victor wasn't Victor anymore but Jake Rivers. He stepped out of the car and turned to help Annie.

Sean slid out and came around. She noted he slipped a hand in his pocket as he walked—a nervous gesture, she thought.

"What's the matter?" she asked Victor as they started toward the door.

She found out before he could answer.

The people at the door froze, staring at them, and then began to whisper furiously.

"Oh dear," she said nervously. She hadn't even thought.

"Yes, I'd say so," Sean replied.

"People tend to recognize us, and I imagine being new at the church here will make us stand out even more," Victor offered.

Annie nodded.

She felt suddenly guilty and embarrassed that she hadn't realized a scene like this might happen.

The man at the door smiled. "Welcome, welcome," he said and reached out to shake each of their hands a bit vigorously. His gaze traveled over her in detail and she felt herself flushing.

"Hello," she said softly. "We're here for church."

"Yes, yes," he replied. Evidently, his English exhausted, he said something apologetically in Dutch.

Sean replied and the man smiled. And then Victor replied and the man absolutely beamed.

"He's glad we understand Dutch," Victor translated, "because the service here is in Dutch."

"Oh dear! The last one was in English. A mission church," she muttered.

Victor chuckled. "I'll translate," he said.

"Or I can if you'd prefer," Sean added.

Annie ignored him and walked in to find every person in the church had turned and was staring at them. "This is not good," she muttered.

"Relax, Annie," Victor said.

She felt like a bug under a microscope. Some of the people looked them up and down and then turned away as if ignoring them. Others whispered in little groups.

She felt so conspicuous and guilty that she'd talked the men into coming with her.

People came up and started talking to Sean and Victor. Both were gracious and smiled, replying in Dutch. Some parishioners spoke in English, though it was so accented she had a hard time understanding it.

Finally the music started, and the pastor called from the front.

Sean's eyebrows shot up.

Victor's hand, which had tightened on her arm, relaxed slightly. "Well. He welcomed us and told everyone to stop treating us as though we walk on water and let us enjoy the service just as they should."

Annie gasped and then giggled. "Oh good."

Victor looked down at her. For the first time it was as if he realized she had been upset and worried. Seeing his attention, her smile faded and she said, "I'm sorry."

He shook his head. "Sean and I both knew what we were getting ourselves in for, putting ourselves out in the public eye. Don't worry. We're big boys.''

She smiled and reached up to squeeze his hand that still covered her arm. ''I—'' she stopped and her eyes widened.

He lifted his head.

She simply shook her head, not believing what she'd almost said. *Love?* No. Not that.

They found seats near the back of the small church and then the singing began.

Victor gaped. ''What are they doing?''

People stood and started clapping, and some were literally jumping while others threw their hands into the air and started shouting.

''Um, well…'' How did she explain to someone who didn't understand about churches like this?

''It looks as if they're having a party,'' Sean said, grinning.

She rolled her eyes and then chuckled. ''Well, I suppose you could say they're partying together.''

''You go to church to have a party?'' Victor asked.

''Not exactly,'' Annie said. Then she gave up. ''Okay. Look at it this way. You just found out someone died for you…you're grateful. So you get excited right?''

Both men looked at her as though she couldn't be serious. ''Well when you watch football or soccer," she said over the music, "don't you get excited when your team does something good?"

"But this isn't football," Victor replied.

"No, it's something much more."

"Well I kinda like it," Sean said. "It's not as stuffy as the places I've gone."

Victor couldn't seem to grasp it. He was watching everyone intently. Annie threw her hands up in frustration and then turned her attention to the overhead projector and phonetically tried to read the words to the very familiar tune. Slowly she caught on—after about the third verse of the song.

Sean, though he didn't sing, grinned a lot, while Victor finally tried to follow the tune. He was very uncomfortable until the slower songs started. Annie noted he knew some of them. Sean even tried singing them, though he kept grinning over at Victor like a total idiot.

What was it with this friendship? She saw in Sean's eyes secrets and knowledge that the two shared. For some reason, she thought, Sean was delighted that Victor was here, though he didn't seem to have an opinion about being here himself.

She didn't understand it.

They had prayer. And unlike in America, their prayer lasted fifteen minutes. She appreciated that Sean leaned over and translated for her quietly.

Then they were seated and the preacher came up to speak.

He again mentioned them, according to Victor. She knew when because both men had those fake smiles on their face again and were nodding and then Victor again muttered something about fame.

Then the pastor went right into preaching.

The sermon was an hour and a half long.

Sean got antsy, but Victor....

She couldn't help but watch Victor as he translated some of the sermon for her and then got so caught up in it that he'd forget to translate, until he saw Sean translating for her. Then he'd immediately start translating again.

His gaze rarely left the pastor.

If he noticed the occasional covert stares from the people around them, he never showed it.

Sean had that smile on his face that said he saw the reactions.

When the sermon was over, they turned to leave—and were nearly mobbed.

People came up to shake their hands and talk to them.

She was surprised that some acted as if they knew them intimately, but the general greetings were normal for a church.

Still, when others started asking for autographs she was flummoxed.

Sean and Victor didn't complain, but signed pieces of paper, church bulletins and such, and chatted amicably with those who approached them.

Amazingly enough, it was the pastor who saved them. He came up, hooked an arm around Victor's shoulders and started toward a small room.

"He wants to chat with us," Sean said.

"Come on," Victor added and grabbed Annie's arm.

The others standing around nodded and smiled and waved and then turned away into little groups.

In English, the pastor said, "I am sorry for the people's reaction. You must admit, it's quite an excitement to have celebrities in our midst. If you make it a common occurrence, I'm sure they'll calm down."

Victor smiled politely. "I enjoyed the message."

Sean shot Annie a wisecracking grin.

The pastor nodded. "We'll go out through my office. I want to give you a card. If you ever need anything, just call."

"Thank you. I don't regularly attend church," Victor said and watched the pastor.

"Ah, well, now it's my duty to tell you that you should. Not necessarily here if you don't find this to your liking, but somewhere." The pastor offered him a large grin, his thinning gray and brown hair falling down into one eye. He swept it back. Going to his desk he found a business card. "Let me know if you ever need anything."

He turned to Sean and handed him a card. "You too."

Finally he looked at Annie. "You don't speak Dutch."

She shook her head. "I'm American."

The pastor shook her hand. "Well, God bless you."

The man chatted a few more minutes in Dutch until the pastor was sure that they could easily get to their car. "I really have to get back to make sure the deacons finished up the counting of the offering and have locked up everything and then I'm sure my wife is waiting. Again, if you need anything…"

Victor said something in Dutch.

The pastor smiled and opened the door.

They exited and walked to the car.

Annie shook her head. "What?" Victor asked.

"That was certainly an experience."

Sean chuckled. "If you think that was an experience, wait until the premiere."

Annie frowned.

"Thanks, Sean," Victor replied sarcastically.

"What?" Sean asked innocently.

"I'm not sure I'm looking forward to it now," Annie said nervously.

"That's what," Victor replied to Sean.

On the way home, it was quiet until Sean said, "So what did you think, Victor?"

Annie had been staring out of the window, ruminating on the message and the three-ring circus after the service. But at Sean's words her gaze turned to Victor and she realized he'd been just as quiet.

"It was unlike anything I'd ever seen." He glanced down at Annie. "The pastor actually talks about God the same way you do."

"Is that unusual?" Annie asked quietly.

Slowly, Victor nodded. "Very." His expression cleared. "I saw what you thought of it, Sean," Victor replied.

Sean grinned. "It was neat."

"Neat?" Annie winced at the word.

Sean nodded. "I heard one of the kids say that, trying to talk to me in English." He chuckled. "Yeah. I liked it. It sure wasn't boring. And I could actually tolerate the pastor. He's a pretty nice bloke. Mind you, sweetheart, I wouldn't want to make it a career, going to church. It'd ruin my bad-boy reputation."

Annie was a bit distressed at Sean's words. He

obviously saw it for he added, "But for you, I'd do it."

She shook her head. "Going to church, having a relationship with God isn't something you can do for someone else."

Sean shifted a bit uncomfortably, and she actually thought he was at a loss for words.

Victor saved his friend by adding, "We're going to need to focus on the premiere coming up. After lunch, would you mind going over the plans with me?"

Sean nodded. "Sounds good."

Annie was disappointed. She'd hoped for more, but it looked as if the conversation was over.

When they arrived back at the house, however, she was surprised when, after Victor had helped her out of the car, he held her back and allowed Sean to get ahead of them before saying, "Thank you, Annie, for today. That service gave me a lot to think about. And I'm glad you saw that I got to experience it."

She smiled. His words lifted her spirit as nothing else had. Before she could answer though, Sean had noticed their absence and paused at the top of the stairs.

"Are you coming?"

Her smile collapsed. "You know, Victor. I sure did like it a lot better before he arrived."

Victor actually chuckled. "You made my day by saying that, Annie. You have no idea how much."

Their spirits restored, Victor lifted Annie into his arms and carried her up the stairs.

Chapter Eleven

Waiting in her hotel suite for Victor and Sean, Annie thought she was going to be sick.

It had been nearly two weeks since Sean had showed up at Victor's door. Now they were all at a hotel in England waiting for the premiere of their movie. Victor had ordered a private jet and had them flown to London last night. The point was, why hadn't she asked where the premiere was to be?

She'd been busy since the day she'd accepted the invitation. First she'd called her children, who were very upset that she was going to a premiere of some movie with this unknown family. She had forced herself not to let them dampen her spirits, promising she would keep in touch.

Though her daughter, especially, had argued, saying she should come home, Annie had held her ground.

Victor had attempted to take her horse riding on three separate occasions. All they had managed the first time was walking the horse because of the cast. But the second and third time they had been able to ride.

And it had been wonderful. Victor had improvised by finding an old-fashioned open carriage, to which he'd harnessed the horse. He'd helped her up into it and held her close as they'd traveled the countryside.

They'd garnered surprised looks from some, but she hadn't cared. They had ridden for what seemed like hours and she had enjoyed every bit of it. Mainly because Sean hadn't been around.

She really liked Sean, but he seemed to take joy in provoking Victor.

She and Victor had stayed out and watched the sunset the second time. The third time he'd showed her his land and they'd actually brought a picnic.

She had fallen in love with Victor. She knew he had feelings for her. She'd caught the looks he gave her when he thought she wasn't watching, the way his gaze followed her.

Actually, it was very frustrating to have all of these feelings and have the other person stay quiet about his. The first day they'd gone to church together, she'd realized how she felt, though it was only as she'd spent more time with Victor that she'd found she wanted to reveal her feelings. But how could she when he didn't show her how he felt?

She wasn't sure why he was holding back, not saying anything, but she was now certain he did care for her.

She'd had fittings for the custom-made dress and shoes. Because of the special walking cast they'd put on her foot, she could walk, but she couldn't wear a shoe on that foot, a unique one that had been made would fit around her cast and disguise it.

Then there was Sean.

She was beginning to relax around him. She wasn't sure what game he was playing. After that first day, when he'd treated her so outrageously, he'd behaved, except when Victor was around.

Anytime Victor was in the same room, Sean flirted—sometimes outrageously, other times simply covertly.

She was ready to throttle him one moment and then later, when he was being the polite friend of Victor…

Victor.

Victor ignored his friend's actions.

She would have appreciated it if he would have a talk with his friend, but he hadn't, so she just decided this must be how movie stars acted toward everyone.

Still, it did nothing to calm her nerves about tonight. It would have been easier going into this knowing that Sean was going to behave himself.

Perhaps that was why Victor wasn't showing his feelings. Victor had been an absolute gentleman except for those smoldering looks in his eyes that caused her heart to quicken. And then there were the gentle touches and caresses.

In a way, Sean had been a blessing. They talked a lot, and she had learned so much about Victor through their conversations. Victor had been a churchgoer and wanted to believe, she thought. But something about his past made him cynical about God, and he just couldn't find a church, according to Sean. Sean thought of himself as Victor's keeper, a big brother to watch out for him, Annie discovered, proving what Victor said was true. The two were very close.

Annie had a feeling more was going on with Sean than she understood, at least when it came to him revealing things to her about Victor. He watched her when she and Victor were together. Sometimes she thought he was measuring her for his best friend, and then he would flirt with her.

She certainly couldn't concentrate when Victor was touching her. What a problem—to be absolutely bowled over by his touches, which she loved, or to have Sean there so they talked and she didn't have to worry as much about Victor's gentle caresses.

Victor had tried church for a while, a long time ago, she thought, with his parents. His paintings were darker than they had once been.

He was searching.

She had adjusted to being with Victor and Sean to the point that she found herself actually mothering Sean occasionally and scolding him for things he said—to his intense amusement. Even Victor had received a tongue-lashing for forgetting his cook's birthday—to which Victor had simply leaned down and almost kissed her—again— would have had Helga not come into the room. Really, all of these people certainly made sure propriety was kept up. Which was good. But still, she so wanted to express her feelings for Victor, and it was so hard with someone always walking into the room.

She hoped tonight she might have some time with Victor alone. Tonight she would tell him how she felt, if he didn't tell her.

She had come to that decision last night while lying in bed in her suite.

A knock sounded at the door.

She carefully made her way across to the door and pulled it opened.

Her mouth dropped in stunned shock.

Victor stood there, dressed in what had to be a very expensive tux, waiting to be allowed in.

"I take it you like it?" he asked, mildly amused.

"I—wow!" She blushed. He was every bit the movie star now, his hair having been professionally done, his tux the latest style.

She stepped back.

He walked in and then turned to her, taking her hands. "You are a fresh breath of beauty in a world too old and cynical, my dear."

She blushed like a kid. She could feel it going up her cheeks all the way to her hairline.

"Turn for me," he said and circled his finger in the air.

She did. She wore a dreamy mauve ball gown. It draped just off the shoulders and dipped slightly, conservatively, in the front and then flared out over the hips, disguising just how wide they were, in her opinion, and fell in soft folds down around her feet, covering the fact she wore a cast. Matching shoes covered both feet.

"I feel like Cinderella at the ball," she said lightly. "What do you think?"

"*I* am devastated that you aren't attending with me," Sean said walking up to the door.

She stopped turning instantly, she was so surprised by his presence.

"Really?" Reanna drawled, glancing at Annie

and then back at Sean. "And I thought you only had eyes for me."

Her voice was biting, though she smiled when she said it.

Sean, in his impossibly gorgeous tux, immediately turned to Reanna. "Of course I do, love. But still, a man can enjoy looking, can he not?"

"If there is something to look at I suppose."

She felt Victor stiffen next to her. She even noted that Sean's smile faltered for a moment. What had they expected? For this woman to like her? She heard the snippiness behind Reanna Chambers's words but chose to ignore them so as not to embarrass Victor.

"You look lovely," Annie offered sweetly.

"I should, honey. This dress cost me a fortune. That's what a star does, dresses for success."

She heard the implication again. She hadn't dressed well.

Sean's eyes narrowed before his gaze went blank. She'd never seen that look from Sean at Victor's house. It was polite and genteel, but it was as if Sean wasn't there. "Shall we go, princess?" he said to Reanna. "We don't want to be late."

She took his arm and they swept off down the hall.

Victor turned to Annie. "I have to apologize for Reanna's—"

"No. You don't." She placed her hand on his

arm and smiled. "A few catty words aren't going to hurt me. I came to be with you tonight. As long as you're happy, nothing else matters."

"I beg to differ," Victor said. "Your happiness is all that matters to me." He grinned.

Then he sobered. "About Sean—"

She shook her head. "Don't worry."

"He can be quite a pain sometimes, but he really is a friend."

"Riding in the car with that woman is going to be interesting," Annie said and took his arm.

"I think you'll find Sean has plucked her wings by now. He was not very happy with what Reanna said to you."

"Oh." She hadn't been sure. She could only read what Sean allowed her to read. He was very good at hiding his emotions when he wanted. She could read Victor, however, and he actually sounded a bit put out with Sean.

She carefully balanced herself against him and together they started down the hall. "I want to tell you how much this vacation has meant to me," she said quietly. "I still can't believe I'm in London."

He grinned. "I told you staying eight weeks would be great."

"Four weeks," she said. "I agreed to four weeks so we could finish that tour."

He grinned. "But you don't want to disappoint your friends by leaving early."

She sighed and couldn't help an exasperated laugh. "I told my friends *two* weeks and I only agreed to *four* weeks for you."

He grinned. "I can still work on you for those last four weeks."

"I have to admit the fields of tulips were something to experience," she said. "And visiting the dikes, and then there was Amsterdam."

He chuckled. "Very...different."

She nodded. She had been stunned as she'd walked down the streets. Eventually she'd stopped looking and kept her gaze directly ahead of her.

The elevator was just expelling some guests so they entered.

Victor slipped his arm around her and hugged her close. "What is that perfume you wear?" he whispered, lowering his nose into the loose strands of hair that curled gently around her face.

Her breathing shortened. He felt so good to lean back into like this. "Magnolia Musk," she replied huskily.

She hadn't realized just how much she'd missed someone else's touch until she'd met this man. Her own soul felt empty and starved until he touched her, and he had the ability to fulfill her secret longings when he held her like this. She had begun to look forward to these moments.

"I smelled that on you the first day we met," he said and his lips brushed the edge of her ear as he said that.

"I like it," she replied low.

The elevator door dinged and opened.

Victor lifted his head, and, of course, met the surprised look of Sean who stood there with Reanna, waiting.

Oh great, Annie thought as Victor stepped to her side and placed her hand on his arm. Sean's grin spread knowingly. But instead of flirting, he said, "Shall we go?"

Every time he had seen Victor doing something like that, he usually decided to flirt. Maybe Reanna had stopped that.

She looked mightily ticked as her gaze slipped over Annie. She turned, took Sean's arm and marched regally out to the limo.

Reanna's sudden smile as she approached the doors was a transformation. Annie was a bit stunned. Reanna looked for all the world like a sweet, loving woman who absolutely oozed affection toward the adoring fans.

Annie wasn't ready for what happened when they stepped out however.

Dozens of paparazzi were waiting and began snapping pictures of them the minute they exited the hotel. They all shouted questions at once. Victor smiled and waved and she took her cue, smiling, though she imagined she looked like a deer caught in the headlights of an oncoming lethal car.

And, that fast, it was over. They were swept into the limo and off they went.

"I hate those people," Reanna complained now. "Someone should take them out and—"

"Now, now, dear," Sean said, smiling and patting her hand. "Free press and all."

"Are you all right?" Victor asked, leaning into Annie and asking very quietly.

She smiled up at Victor. "It's a bit overwhelming. How do you put up with that all the time?"

He smiled. "It's good for the business," he replied.

"And it keeps our faces in front of the fans," Sean added.

Reanna tapped her foot. "Still, they have no respect, Sean. How you can be so patient with them…"

She trailed off and then gave Sean a look that Annie wished she'd missed. "However, if you can put up with it, I'll put up with it for you."

Victor, who had his back slightly to Reanna, simply rolled his eyes.

Annie laughed.

She immediately regretted it as all gazes turned toward her. "What was that about?" Reanna demanded.

"I was telling her a joke," Victor said, mildly.

"A very private joke," he said and lowered his voice.

"I'll bet," said Sean. The twinkle was back in his eyes, and she had a feeling Sean knew exactly what Victor had done. He gave her a warm smile before turning his attention back to his date.

He really was a nice guy, she thought.

The limo pulled to a stop. "Before we get out, here are a few guidelines. Smile. Nod. Don't answer any questions about personal relationships or where you are from and above all, don't give them your name. Simply say, 'I'm with Jake.'"

She laughed nervously. "What if they ask something that those answers don't cover?"

"I'll help deflect the press, sweetheart," Sean said.

"Oh, please," Reanna said, obviously upset that Sean's attention wasn't completely on her. "She's at least forty. She can take care of herself."

Sean gave Reanna a look that sent her into a pout.

Victor's gaze was strained. But the door was opened at that moment. "Here we go," he said.

He stepped out and Annie followed.

She nearly staggered from the noise alone. Huge crowds were on each side of the walkway. Cameras immediately started going off and reporters shouted questions. Victor managed to slip from side to side to sign autographs as they walked and somehow Sean always managed to be on the opposite side of her when Victor moved. He too was signing autographs. Reanna was acting like a queen, signing, posing and answering questions thrown to her from the crowd.

Annie heard Victor deflecting questions about her, instead saying, "She's a friend. Give us a break. You'll find out soon." And other things like that, all the while showing his perfect charming self to the people around.

And then they were inside. Victor patted her hand. "I need you to stand right over here," he said, leading her away from the cameras, "while I do a few interviews and then we can go into the theater. Okay?"

She nodded. "Thank you. It'll be nice to catch my breath."

He smiled. "You're doing great."

He squeezed her hand and then walked off.

Sean sauntered over to her, having just finished an interview. Reanna was still being asked questions about a movie of hers that had just come out last week.

"How are you holding up, sweetheart?"

She glanced sideways at Sean. "It's overwhelming, actually."

He nodded. "I don't know if you ever get used to it. You do learn to deal with it, however. Of course, there are some, like Reanna, who thrive on it. But when something happens and she gets sour publicity, I imagine, she too, will take a new look at it.''

"Sour publicity? Oh.'' She suddenly remembered Sean being blamed for the break-up of someone's marriage.

"I've had several bouts of it. That's what happens as you rise in the ranks of stardom. The job becomes a monster, fed by the adoring fans and press. But then, without them, you wouldn't make money doing a job you love.''

"You know, Sean, I think you're not at all what you seem,'' Annie said, quite sagely.

He glanced at her. "Oh, I'm what I seem all right, but then, right now in public I can't show you that.''

She gaped at his words. "You're flirting with me for a reason, and I'm not sure what...''

He shook his head. "You haven't figured it out yet?'' He nodded, his gaze boring into her own. "I'll have to fix that, I suppose.''

Her eyes widened. "I'm not sure I like the sound of that.''

"Oh, you might not, but I guarantee you'll like the results.'' She was certain he wasn't talking about him, but she couldn't quite figure out his hidden meaning. He was definitely up to something.

Victor chose that moment to return and the look

he sent Sean was telling. Victor, it seemed, was getting tired of Sean flirting with her. She hadn't thought he'd cared until just now.

She would never figure out Sean. Why would he treat his friend this way? She would have to explain that Sean hadn't meant anything by that last sentence Victor had overheard. She didn't think he had, at least.

"Ready?" Victor asked.

She nodded.

"We'll see you inside, Sean," Victor said.

"Sure thing, Jake. As soon as I can get Reanna away from the cameras."

Together she and Victor entered the darkened theater to watch the showing of *Shelter,* and she wondered how this night would end.

Chapter Twelve

It was 2:00 a.m. and the party that had followed the showing was finally slowing. Annie had met more stars on the ground than there were in the sky tonight. Many had been nice. Some people were curious while others were definitely shocked at her appearance on Jake's arm. She'd heard him called Jake more than she cared to admit. She was even beginning to think of him as Jake—at least in this setting. For the Jake at the party hadn't been the same Victor she'd known at his estate. He'd been 'on' so to speak, socializing, saying all the right things.

Of course, wasn't everyone that way when out around others they weren't close to? She supposed even she was. She certainly had been tonight.

Her jaw hurt from smiling so much.

"Jake wanted me to escort you to the limo. He said he'd be there shortly," Sean said coming up to her.

She glanced around. "Where is Reanna?"

He shrugged. "She's off with someone else. And I can't say that I mind much," he said crisply. "She was quite a bore."

He glanced over her head and saw something. "Come on," he said and took her arm.

Before she could turn around, he'd slipped his arm around her just as Victor would have and had escorted her out of the ballroom where the party had been held.

"So, Victor still hasn't declared himself?" he asked as they walked.

Annie was shocked by Sean's words. "What do you mean?"

He chuckled and propelled her onward. "I imagine he is a bit stubborn, but I had hoped that tonight, with all of the press…still I should have realized he would have to be pushed a bit harder."

"Sean, I'm sorry but I don't understand."

"So, what did you think of the movie?" he asked mildly, changing the subject.

"I enjoyed it," she said, though one part had certainly disturbed her.

"But not all of it, I can tell," Sean said, too wisely.

"No. Well, it's just…"

They passed through the great hall toward the exit. She thought she heard someone call her name.

Sean continued walking, carrying her right along with him. "Seeing an on-screen romance between Jake and the leading lady bothered you, didn't it?"

Her gaze slipped back up to Sean's. "Am I that transparent?" she asked miserably.

Out of all that had happened, that one thing had disturbed her. Probably because all she could think about lately was Victor and wanting to experience his kisses. She was ashamed to admit it, but she had fallen hard and fast for the man and couldn't think of anything but him.

Sean nodded. "I think you are. Of course, I couldn't see Jake's reaction on your other side. Really, sweetheart, it's business. The woman he was kissing is worse than Reanna. And it's hard to get into the mood when you have fifty other people standing around watching. Trust me. There's nothing there between them."

"It looked so real," she said quietly as they pushed through the doors. And she'd seen Meredith. She was gorgeous and perfect. How could he not fall for her?

Most of the paparazzi were gone now. Sean signaled for the attendants to bring the limo around and then strolled off to a secluded area to wait. "It's supposed to look real. The directors keep at it until they get the scenes right. That's the idea behind movies, to make the audience think it's real. And that's the idea behind what I'm about to do," he said gently.

Confused, she glanced up. "I'm sorry. What?"

His gaze turned dark. He said something in Dutch and then, to her utter shock, his hands slipped to her shoulders and he pulled her forward.

"Wha—" she started and was engulfed in his kiss.

Her mind absolutely froze with astonishment for a moment.

Good heavens. Sean Hampton was kissing her, she thought and then her mind began working again. Sean Hampton was *kissing* her!

She lifted her hands to push him away.

"Excuse me."

Before she could move, a hand closed around her upper arm and she was jerked away.

Annie's ball gown tripped her and she staggered. She latched onto the hand holding her and looked up. *Oh good heavens!* Victor stood there, eyes blazing.

Sean lifted his hands in mock surprise. "I didn't think it was serious between you two," he said.

"What?" Disbelieving, she looked back and forth between the two men. She saw flashes and thought, Great, lightning and thunder. Rain was coming and they were standing out here arguing or—something—since she couldn't understand them. Words were exchanged in rapid-fire Dutch, and then the limo arrived.

"Come on," Victor said and hauled her along with him to the limo, shoving her inside, almost causing her to trip again.

"I—" she started.

She glanced back and saw Sean smile at her.

She glared.

Victor climbed in and closed the door and off went the limo. "But what about him?"

Oh boy. That was the wrong thing to ask. Victor's gaze riveted to her.

"Would you rather be with him?" Victor asked. "Is that it?"

"Huh?" Her mouth fell open.

Growling low in his throat, he said, "I've wanted to do this since day one. I guess I should have just done it."

Before she could answer, he'd grabbed her and pulled her into his arms.

It only took a moment for her to melt and accept Victor's kiss.

"Victor," she whispered. She wanted to say so

many things, tell him so many things. Unfortunately, his name was all she could remember.

She couldn't believe how right this felt. She also couldn't believe the emotions he pulled out of her. In his arms like this, she couldn't deny the feelings she had for him. She ran her hands up through his short hair, thinking how much she'd wanted to reach up and do that since she'd met him. It was soft, curly, slick between her fingers. She squeezed her hands closed around it and sighed.

She had grown to care more than just a little for this man. If she were honest, she would admit she could even find hope again of not being alone the rest of her life, of having someone to share it with. She could admit that love was in her heart for Victor Rivers.

Before she could say anything, however, Victor suddenly groaned and released her. Annie still leaned across Victor's lap, staring up at him in utter wonder.

She touched her lips and simply blinked.

"You were kissing Sean."

"What!"

Shocked at his abrupt words, she struggled to sit up.

Though Victor looked angry, his hands were gentle as they helped her back across to her own seat.

"You heard me," he said shortly.

"I wasn't!" she argued, abruptly pulled out of the haze Victor had managed to weave in her mind.

Victor's eyes narrowed. "I saw you."

"No, you didn't," Annie argued and started to get angry. "You saw *him* kissing me."

He shook his head. "After the way you looked at him the day he arrived? I heard what he said to you. He's been infatuated since day one. He even told me he was going to chase you."

"He what?" Flabbergasted, she simply stared at him.

"When he first arrived. He said he was interested. And you haven't rebuked his advances. And then tonight you left with him and went to the limo, willingly going into his arms."

"I did not. Victor, what is the matter with you!" This was not the man she'd come to love, was it?

Victor fell back in his seat. He lifted his hands to his head and ran them into his hair. "Sean is driving me crazy chasing you as he has been."

She shook her head. "He's not chasing me."

"What would you call it?" he demanded.

"I don't know."

"You wanted him to come back with us in the limo."

"No," she said, working hard to keep her voice

calm. "I just thought since he rode with us, it was impolite to leave him standing on the sidewalk."

"He lives here, remember?"

"No, Victor, I don't remember. I had no idea he lived in London."

He sighed. He looked absolutely miserable.

She wasn't sure what to say. Slowly, she began, "He told me you had asked him to escort me to the limo."

"Why would I do that?"

"I don't know, Victor. Because you are good friends."

"Why would he lie to you?"

She shrugged. "He's been acting oddly all week. The reason I didn't rebuke him at your house, Victor, is that I'm not used to being around people like you. I wasn't sure if what he was doing was considered normal banter. You never said anything about it."

"I'm not your boss. If you want to flirt with him or allow him to flirt with you, it's not my say."

Annie was hurt. "He only flirts when you're around. The rest of the time he's a perfect gentleman, except for tonight."

"Sean's not that way. You obviously wanted more from him than you're admitting."

Annie's eyes suddenly widened. "You're jealous."

He glanced up. "No. I'm not. I don't believe in long-term relationships. I'm the type that believes in enjoying what you have, and when the other person is done having fun, you split."

Annie gasped.

His words caused her physical pain.

"So, that's all this friendship has been to you?"

He shrugged. "I admit it's been fun, but if you want him…"

"I keep telling you, I don't!" She couldn't believe she said that. Before she'd met Victor, the idea of ever kissing someone as handsome and well-known as Sean Hampton had been a dream as it was for every woman in America, and England as well, most likely the world. But since she'd met Victor, Sean had paled in comparison.

Victor obviously read her thoughts in her gaze, because he actually looked upset.

"You can't see past your jealousy," Annie said simply.

"Please," he said and waved a hand.

"I'm right. That's what Sean meant tonight."

"What?"

She shook her head. "You're unwilling to listen."

The limo pulled up to the hotel. Victor got out. "The plane is waiting to take us back to Holland.

I won't be on it tonight, however. Make yourself at home when you return.''

He closed the door.

She gasped again. What was that all about? Before she could get out and confront him, the limo pulled away from the curb. She fell back against the seat, aghast.

Victor had dumped her—in England—alone.

The man she'd come to love had simply stepped out of the limo and sent her on her way to the airport. Annie burst into tears. Good heavens. She cried all the way to the airport.

At the airport the driver pulled around to a private entrance. She didn't even have her clothes from the hotel. What was she going to do about them?

They sat there for at least fifteen minutes before the driver got out. He came around and opened the door.

She stepped out—and came face-to-face with Sean Hampton.

She didn't think, only reacted. With every bit of anger and pain in her, she reared back and slapped the fire out of him.

Sean actually staggered.

''Whoa!'' he said, grabbing his cheek.

She started toward him and he grabbed her hands. ''Calm down, sweetheart—''

"Don't call me that!"

"No really. Where is Victor? I came to apologize. He left so fast—"

"He left me."

She started sobbing again.

"What?" He said a very British curse and then looked back at her. "That wasn't supposed to happen. I was going to give him some time to come to grips—"

"I don't want to hear it."

Her shoulders drooped and she started crying again. "Uh, Annie. We need to get you on the plane. The paparazzi are coming."

"I don't care," she said miserably.

"Well I do, and Victor will, eventually." He slipped an arm around her and picked her up.

"What are you doing? Keep your hands off me."

"My lands, woman, will you calm down? I'm only trying to help you," he said sternly.

"Just like when you kissed me?"

"That was fun," he said cheekily and then immediately backpedaled when she started to struggle. "I'm sorry. No. That was a mistake. I hadn't realized just how deep...oh for crying out loud. Stop struggling!"

When she continued to struggle he squeezed her

tightly against him. "You're not a size three, you know. I might actually drop you!"

She gasped.

He reddened. "I didn't mean that how it sounded. Please, Miss Hooper. Let me explain."

They arrived at the plane, and he lowered her to her feet.

Looking up she saw nowhere to go but up, so she simply started climbing the stairs. Which was really difficult in a full-length gown.

"I'm only helping," Sean warned as he reached around her and helped gather some of the dress into his hands.

"Thank you," she said stiffly, wishing she could slam the door in his face when she finally made it onto the plane.

He released her dress.

She glanced back, hoping to see that Victor was somehow there. He wasn't however.

She stepped inside the plane. Going to a seat she collapsed down into it.

Sean showed up shortly and offered her brandy.

"I don't drink."

"Ah. That's right. Sorry." Going back to the refrigerator, he looked in and brought back a bottle of water. "Here, sweetheart. Drink this."

"Don't call me sweetheart," she muttered and accepted the water.

Sean seated himself across the aisle from her. "Buckle up, love," he said softly. "We're about to take off."

She gave up arguing with him. Listlessly she pulled the seat belt around her waist and snapped it.

He snapped his own seat belt.

In seconds they felt the plane taxi to take off.

She closed her eyes and laid her head back. Absently she realized most of her hair had come out of the pins and was loose around her face.

She reached up and touched it.

"I see you and Victor had a...talk."

Fresh tears slipped down her cheeks.

"I'm so sorry, love," he said low. "I really didn't mean for this to happen." He reached across to her hand and pressed his hankie into her hand.

The plane lifted into the air. She held her breath until they leveled off and then she opened her eyes.

"Tell me, Sean. If you didn't mean for this to happen then why did you kiss me?"

Chapter Thirteen

Sean sighed. He looked more serious than she'd ever seen him. "It was because he was lying to himself."

Annie only blinked.

Sean thought about how to explain this. He knew so much about his friend, Jake, but... "You realize Victor is in love with you?"

Fresh tears spilled over Annie's cheeks.

What a sticky wicket, Sean thought, frustrated.

"You purposely tried to ruin that?" The words came out strained, through a tight throat. Sean took the hankie and dabbed at her face.

She shook her head no, but then accepted the hankie as he slipped it back into her hand.

"I called, planning to come up a few weeks ago,

the day after you'd been in the accident. Something about Victor's attitude sounded strange.

"I stayed away for a few days but decided to come on up. Jake and I go way back to the beginning when I was young in the business. We've been in half a dozen movies together. We're close."

"What does this have to do—"

Sean clasped his hands in front of him. "Let me explain, please, Annie."

She nodded and wiped at her eyes.

"He was running from God. I'm not so religious, you understand, but Victor, he is. Only someone who really believes in God could be so angry at God."

"Is that so?" Annie asked quietly, studying Sean now.

How did she do that? Victor said she'd been looking into his soul the entire time she was there. He shifted uncomfortably. "We're not talking about me, sweetheart. Anyway, he tried a few churches but just couldn't reconcile what happened with his family and his anger at church. He lived wild, which was fine with me at the time because I was a bit of a wild buck too. Eventually, however, it started affecting his work. I felt it my responsibility to take him under my wing. I was the more experienced. And it's been that way ever since. We're friends, but I tend to play big brother to him, even though he's older than I am.

"I noticed about a year and a half ago a change in him. He started spending more time in Holland—that's where he goes to escape the world. His painting became dark and his poetry searching.

"When I showed up and saw you pray at the meal, I realized then what was different. He'd found the counter to his parents. You weren't bitter and angry.

"His parents were something else," Sean said and cast a disgusted glance her way. "I've met them a couple of times and they are not happy people. You, instead, glowed whenever you talked about God, and when you took us to that little church…"

She sniffed. "I'm sorry for how they treated you."

He shook his head. "People get used to it after a while and you find out who are and are not your real friends. Jake knows I'm his real friend. He'll get over this with me."

At her frown he held up a hand. "Anyway, that afternoon when we were talking, Victor said he didn't date girls like you, he'd sworn off good girls because he didn't believe in forever after."

She nodded. "He told me that in the limo," she whispered painfully.

Sean actually hurt for her. He had blown it big-time. He hadn't thought his friend would actually stay behind in London and send the woman he loved back to Holland alone. He had planned for them to be on the plane, not him. He hadn't planned to go back to Holland for a few days, to give them time to work out their feelings.

Boy, had he messed things up. "He may say that, but with you, love, he doesn't mean it." He reached out and took her hand trying to comfort her.

Amazingly enough, she didn't attack him, but gripped his hand in return. She had to be really hurting to do that, he thought, ashamed.

"One thing is certain, I knew my silly games could make Jake jealous. I was hoping I could prod him into admitting his feelings for you and then you two could go from there. I really thought he'd declare himself, but when he hadn't tonight, well, I wanted him to realize he couldn't lose you, that he couldn't go on without you."

"By kissing me?"

Sean shrugged. "It seemed like a good idea at the time." He flushed a bit.

Annie sighed and released her hand. She wrapped her arms around herself, huddling down and withdrawing from the world around her.

Sean got up and moved into the seat next to her.

Carefully, he placed an arm around her. She didn't fight, so he pulled her closer, but not with any ill intentions this time.

"I am so sorry, Annie. I was a cad, to say the least. I guess there is still something cynical in me that says there really isn't a woman like you out there."

"What do you mean?" she asked, but didn't change her position. She was still stiff and huddled down into herself.

"I mean a woman who believes in love and happily ever after. All of the women I know have Jake's opinion."

She loosened up a bit. "You don't, do you?"

He sighed. After what he'd caused, he should be honest with her. "I guess I'm really a romantic at heart. I hope that one day, out there, maybe there will be a woman for me who will love me for who I am, not what I am."

Slowly, she nodded.

"I thought I'd found that with Victor," she whispered and fresh tears spilled down her cheeks.

He gently pulled until she came over into his arms. She was so trusting and forgiving. How could he ever have doubted that she was a good person and really cared for his friend?

"Shush, sweetheart," he said and rubbed his hand up and down her back. "I'll find a way to fix this. The point I was making is that I was trying to get Victor to realize he cared and at least make some sort of move on you to return your love.''

''Well he did that…for all of about two minutes. Then your name came up. I think he was only kissing me because you kissed me.''

Sean considered that. ''Maybe, darling, but think about this. It may have started out that way, but Victor never does anything he doesn't want to do. It'll only take him a few days to realize what an idiot he's been, he may have already discovered his mistake, and then he'll come after you.''

She shook her head against his chest. ''It's too late.''

''How can you say that?'' he asked, trying to convince her otherwise. ''I'm telling you, he's in love with you. He saw hope in you. The other night after church we spoke while you were in bed. He actually admitted there might be something to Christianity after all. I laughed. I mean, well, that sounded so funny coming from him since he's been running so long, but then…''

He paused. ''He has to come to terms with that before he can go on. And he'll be forced to come to terms with that now because his honor won't let him come to you until he does.''

''What do you mean by that?''

Sean rested his chin on top of her head. He could

feel her shudders as she tried to get her tears under control. "He thinks of you as a 'good girl.' He wouldn't make a move on you because of that. He has now done that and that experience won't leave him. Eventually, he's going to realize how he feels about you as he goes over what happened in his mind and why he was so upset over the kiss he saw."

She stiffened slightly.

"He'll have to face that you love God. He always told me someone who loved God had to have God first in their life. He knows God is first in your life. If he can't come to terms with that then he won't be able to come to you."

"But you don't understand, Sean," Annie said and leaned back to look up into his eyes. "He can't come to God because of *me*. He has to change in his heart because he wants to, regardless of me."

"But why?" Sean asked, not understanding and already having heard this once from Annie.

She sighed. "Christianity is a relationship with someone. Could you start up a relationship with me and sustain it just because Victor dumped me?"

Sean shook his head. "Of course not. Guilt would probably tear us apart within the first month."

"It's the same with God. If he decides to go to

church simply because I'm a Christian then he's doing it because of me, not because of God, just like you'd be dating me because of guilt from what happened with Victor not because you were attracted to me.''

Sean was surprised. He'd never thought about Christianity that way. "I've always considered Christianity a church thing."

She shook her head. "It's an intimate relationship with another person that requires communication and a willingness to obey and give."

"I don't understand," Sean said simply. "But we're getting off the subject. What I am saying is that Victor will have to face his problems now. I expected him to do that with you. He's chosen solitude which I should have realized he'd do. And for that I apologize, but please, Annie, give him time. Give him a chance to sort through his feelings."

She sighed. Finally, she moved to sit up straight. He released her.

"You really care about him, don't you, Sean?"

He met her eyes. "I do."

"And you really thought you were doing right."

He nodded. "I can't apologize enough for the outcome."

"I understand now what you meant about doing

your job. You were hoping to trigger something in Victor.''

"I am truly sorry."

She nodded and then closed her eyes. "I need a nap. I'm going to snooze while we fly, if you don't mind."

What could he say?

He reached up and signaled the attendant who turned the lights out for them. He allowed her darkness while he held her hand and debated how he was going to clean up this mess.

Of course, Annie wasn't really asleep. She was wondering how the man who had caused her so much trouble had suddenly become her confidant.

What would Victor say about that?

He'd laughed at the way the two had traded barbs. He'd also been jealous, she now realized, of the way they had traded barbs. The only problem was that her barbs weren't in fun. They were an attempt to deter Sean's attraction. He hadn't been attracted, however, he'd simply been trying to make Victor jealous.

He had succeeded, far beyond his wildest imaginings.

If Victor was jealous, he had to care. But, then, as she'd known from the beginning, he wasn't serving God. He'd told her once that he'd given his heart to God several years ago, but he'd long ago forsaken him, running as far and fast as he could.

What do I do, Father? she silently asked.

Peace touched her heart and she heard *Trust in me*.

A love she'd never felt burned in her heart for the man, but she couldn't marry him if he wasn't on the same page as she was.

Marriage?

Why was she even thinking about that? He surely wasn't.

Dear God I thought that maybe you had sent me here to change his heart? Was I wrong?

And then, slowly, it dawned on her. She was the one who had changed. She'd been shy and afraid to leave her own home since her husband had died. And yet, here she was on a plane with a man of world renown. Before coming on vacation to Holland, she probably would have fainted dead away if something like this had happened.

Maybe God had a bigger plan than she could see. After all, it was true a person could only see through a glass darkly. Maybe there was more going on that she knew.

She sighed.

''We're nearly home.''

She jumped at Sean's words so close to her ear. Had she been daydreaming that long?

She opened her eyes and realized they were descending.

When they landed, Sean reached over to help her with her seat belt.

"What are you doing?" Surprised Annie pulled back slightly.

Sean smiled. "Watching out for my best friend's girl," he tried to joke and Annie realized he was trying to cheer her. And his words worked, to a point.

Annie actually laughed. "I don't think so, Sean. I seriously doubt he wants you watching out for me. If he knew you were in the plane, he'd probably disown you."

"Oh, I'm sure he knows by now, darling. I called from the plane and when he didn't answer, I left him a message with a few choice Dutch words explaining where I would be."

She groaned as she imagined what Sean must have said, and then thought of something else. Turning to him, she said, "Speaking of Dutch, what did you say to him back at the party?"

He smiled. The door opened and he helped her up and preceded her down the stairs. "I told him he was in love with you when I called him. *Jij bent verliefd op haar,*" he repeated. "And then that you loved him and he needed to get his head…well, suffice to say I became very British with what I suggested.''

"But what did you say to him when he came out of the hotel?''

He grinned. "I didn't say anything to him, sweetheart. It was directed to you.''

"And that was?''

He shifted. "You won't like it.''

"And that was?'' she repeated.

"Just what I wanted to do when we got back to the hotel.''

He was right. She didn't like it. "He said you were driving him crazy with all of the flirting.''

"Oh my dear, I knew that when I arrived. You do know what you said to me, don't you?''

Annie thought back to that day and realized a suddenly bad feeling was creeping up on her. "I said 'welcome,' right?''

He shook his head and laughed. At the last step he turned and accepted her hand to help her down the last two steps. "You said, 'I'm his.' ''

"I *what?*'' Aghast, she simply stared.

"Oh, yes. I knew right then that you were more to him than a simple friend. He'd fooled himself by repeating that bit about friendship over and over.''

"I wonder what else he's taught me in Dutch that means something else.''

"Well, you did tell me a couple of times *Ga weg*."

She tried to remember when and shook her head.

"When he was irritated with me he'd feed you that as an answer. It actually means, Go away."

She groaned.

He laughed.

They piled into the car. She pulled her dress in and put on her seat belt. Reaching down, she removed the shoe from her broken foot. She held it up. "He had these made especially for me because he didn't want someone seeing my bare foot and realizing I wore a cast."

"Good grief," he said looking at the shoe. "It looks like a hobbit's foot."

"Hobbit?" she asked.

"You've never read J. R. R. Tolkien?"

When she shook her head he groaned. "I'll find you a copy in Victor's collection when we get back to the estate and you can while away the rest of your vacation reading."

She shook her head. "You're as bad as Victor there. I haven't said I'm going to stay."

He turned onto the main highway that led into the small town of Haut. She laid her shoe down by her feet.

"You really shouldn't leave until this is solved."

"I'm not the one who left. I was pushed away," she reminded him. "Besides, isn't it true that Cinderella turns into a pumpkin at midnight? And it's way past midnight."

"Her coach does," Sean corrected. "Just give Victor time," he added.

She didn't answer, and in minutes they were through the town and at the estate.

Wearily she climbed out of the car. He strolled in front of the car and stopped by her side, slipping an arm around her.

She glared but he only smiled. "Friends. Pax, darling. I'm being honest when I say I have no designs on you. My heart belongs to Victor and what is best for him."

She relaxed and accepted his help.

Slowly, she climbed the stairs. At the top she allowed him to open the door—and was stunned by the scene.

"Where is my dad?" A young boy came storming across the foyer, anger and desperation in every step.

His gaze was on Sean. "Uncle Sean? Is Dad with you?"

The boy was crying. This had to be Victor's son. He had the same brandy-colored eyes and his face looked just like Victor's, though he had light-golden hair.

Sean turned his attention to the boy, releasing Annie. "Hello, Josh. No. I'm afraid not. He's still in London. What's the matter?"

"I hate him. I hate my mom." He rubbed his nose and then cried, "I ran away from home."

With that he turned and rushed toward the library.

Sean simply stared.

Annie thought, of all the times for Victor to be gone, this had to be the worst. Obviously, something had come to a head with his mom and he needed his parent.

And his dad was in London, angry with Annie.

This was all her fault.

Chapter Fourteen

"I'd better call Victor," Sean said.

Annie agreed. "I'll go see if I can talk to Josh."

She walked around the scattered mess in the foyer—there was a skateboard, a suitcase, a fishing pole and a backpack alongside a bedroll.

She was careful not to trip as she made her way across the room. She tapped lightly on the library door.

She heard the young boy sniffling. She stepped inside. The library was larger than the parlor, but not by much. Books of all types lined the shelves and there was dark leather furniture. A library of the type you'd find in an old Regency mystery.

The boy stood by the books. He had just started pulling them out and throwing them.

Appalled, she crossed the room. "Mr. Rivers. Stop that right now."

The authority in her voice stopped him in his tracks. He glanced at her. "Who are you?"

She hesitated and then walked forward, holding out her hand. "I'm Annie Hooper. And you are?"

"Josh Rivers." He obediently took her hand.

"I take it your dad didn't know you were coming tonight?"

He shook his head and wiped at his eyes, embarrassed. She motioned toward the sofa. "Want to talk?"

He eyed her suspiciously. "Do you know Uncle Sean?"

She thought, if you only knew kid. "As a matter of fact, I do. We're friends."

He snorted.

"You find that hard to believe?"

He shrugged, sullen.

"I thought you were at your mom's?"

"I wanted to come visit," he said, and she could tell only a good upbringing kept him from leaving the room.

"You told Uncle Sean you'd run away," she said softly.

He didn't comment.

"Were there problems, Josh?"

He shrugged. "Mom got married today."

"Oh dear," she said softly.

Fresh tears filled his eyes. He stiffened. "I heard him tell Mom he didn't want a kid. She said she was going to talk to Dad. I just figured I'd save her the talk."

Appalled, she couldn't help but stare. "Oh, Josh," she said softly.

The boy started crying again. He threw himself into her arms. Being a mother, she gladly accepted him and stroked his hair. He cried as if he'd lost part of himself today. And he probably had.

She saw Sean open the door and then stop—surprise in his eyes. She motioned him to stay quiet by shaking her head and he entered, staying in the background.

"If your dad had known that, he would have flown to get you himself. He's missed you so much. He was very upset when your mom wouldn't let him come get you early."

"How do you know?" he asked through the tears.

"I was here. He was frustrated. Tell me," she asked softly, "did she want you to stay because of the marriage?"

He shook his head. "She doesn't want to lose the child support. They had a big fight about that. That was why she wasn't marrying him. But he said he could support her fine."

Anger flashed. Annie felt it. Her entire face flooded with heat, she was so angry. "Well, your dad won't feel that way. I can just about guarantee you that you'll have a place here. He's missed you terribly."

"Then why wasn't he here? He said to call, and I called and he wasn't here."

"Oh, honey," she said and looked up at Sean. "He had a premiere tonight."

"He sure did, sport," Sean finally said, coming over. "We flew to London. Your dad had some unfinished business. I put a call in and as soon as he gets it, he'll call."

The phone rang as if on cue.

Sean didn't wait for one of the staff to pick up the phone but instead reached for it.

"Hello?"

There was a pause and then Victor's tones could be heard on the other end. Sean switched to another language and quickly explained the situation. She wasn't sure what language he spoke, but when he was done, he handed the phone to Josh.

Annie stood and crossed the room to give Josh some privacy. Sean followed.

"How many languages do you speak?" Annie asked.

"Spanish, French, English, Dutch and German. I guess that'd be five."

"And that language was?"

"Spanish," he said. "I wanted to tell him what happened without Josh hearing. Josh speaks Dutch."

"Am I the only person who doesn't speak more than one language?" she asked frustrated.

He smiled. "You're American," he said easily.

She growled.

"Victor asked if you were okay," Sean said.

"What did you tell him?"

He shrugged. "That you missed him, and he was a jerk to make you ride the plane home, and then I apologized. I told him we would talk about this later, that his son needed him now."

"And?"

"He's still upset. I don't think he'd be coming home if Josh wasn't here."

She sighed. Sean took her hands. "Don't lose heart, Annie."

Josh finally hung up the phone. Annie moved back across the room and sat down on the sofa. "You feel better now?"

He shrugged. "Dad's on his way home. He said he'd be here sometime in the morning, around 7:00 a.m. or so."

Annie reached over and stroked the young boy's neck. "You want some cocoa and then maybe some sleep so you can be up and ready to talk to him when he arrives?''

The boy was tired. His shoulders drooped and his eyes looked as if he'd been crying on and off all day.

''I s'pose,'' he said.

She stood, with Sean's help and then slipped her arm around the boy. She'd been on this leg too much today and it was really beginning to ache.

''What's the matter with you?'' Josh asked studying the stiff way she moved.

''I have a broken leg,'' she replied.

''Yeah?'' The boy's interest perked.

She walked slowly along.

''Your dad did it, sport,'' Sean said with relish.

''Really?'' The boy's eyes rounded.

''We were in a car accident,'' she explained and shot a look askance at Sean.

''I'll tell you all about it—later,'' Sean said and gave the boy a look that said, girls just don't understand these things.

She rolled her eyes. ''Men,'' she muttered.

Once in the kitchen she searched and found the cocoa and made up two cups. She honestly didn't feel like drinking any, but Sean seemed to be doing well with the boy so she thought they'd probably drink theirs together.

Bringing the two cups over, she set them down

in front of them. Sean glanced up at her. "You might want to clean the cocoa off the dress you're wearing."

She glanced down. "Oh dear." She brushed at it.

He shook his head. "On second thought, that dress cost quite a penny, you'd better leave it to the professionals. Doing that is smearing it in."

"Just how much did this cost?" she asked suspiciously, but she did stop batting at the fine covering she'd spilled on it.

He named the amount and she nearly fell over.

"They don't make dresses that expensive, do they?" Good heavens. If she'd known Victor had spent that much on the dress, she never would have allowed it. That was more than she'd spent on her entire wedding.

He shook his head. "That and more sometimes."

"I'm going upstairs to change. Excuse me please."

She turned and, muttering to herself, she left the kitchen. Crossing to the elevator she stepped in and went up to the upper level. This entire night had been a fiasco. From her encounter with Victor to the flight home and then meeting Victor's son. And now finding out she'd messed up a dress worth more than her former husband had made in a year.

Life couldn't get any worse, she thought miserably.

Going into her room, she started peeling the dress off only to hear the phone ring.

Now what?

It was probably Victor telling her to vacate the premises. She picked it up, beating the maid to it.

"Hello?"

"Mama Annie?"

It was her daughter. "Susan. Hello." This was a surprise.

"I'm pregnant."

She dropped to the edge of her bed, stunned. "What?"

Her daughter burst into tears. "It's all your fault. And I'm going to have an abortion."

Oh, good heavens. Annie reeled in shock. "Susan, you are not." She worked hard to stay calm and talk to her daughter. "Talk to me."

"How could you leave us? When I needed you most you're out gallivanting all over the world. And now I have no one here."

"Susan?" Her daughter was crying hysterically. "Susan," she said calmly. "What is it?"

"We just saw you on TV. You were kissing Sean Hampton. How could you? I need you here, and you're in London!"

"How in the world could you know that? It only happened a few hours ago."

"It was on TV, Annie!" She always dropped the "Mama" when she was angry.

The flashes she'd thought were lightning. They hadn't been that at all, but cameras. She felt like an idiot, so naive and out of touch with this world.

"You've forgotten us and you're out running wild with some man. And who was the man who grabbed you? Oh, yes," she heard Susan's brother in the background. "Jake Rivers. You were with them. How Daddy ever loved you I don't know. Mom always said you were nothing but trash. I didn't believe her, until now."

That was like a slap in the face to Annie—and it brought reality crashing home. She had been gallivanting around while leaving her kids to fend for themselves. Guilt assailed her.

"Susan, you can't mean that," she said.

"You're not here are you?" she countered.

In that moment, Annie made her decision. "I'll be home tomorrow. Do not do anything rash until I can get there and talk."

She hesitated.

"Susan?"

Finally she answered. "Okay."

Susan hung up the phone.

Annie slowly replaced the receiver.

Tears filled her eyes. But this time they didn't fall. Instead, she switched into a pair of pants and a top and began packing.

Chapter Fifteen

Victor was exhausted and had just arrived at his house. It was seven-thirty in the morning.

He'd had too many hours to think about what happened. Why had he let Sean upset him so? He realized now Sean had simply done it to get Victor's attention.

He'd gotten it all right.

But to send Annie away as he had.

He admitted it was an excuse. He'd been getting too close to her and it had scared him. Big-time. The last church service they had gone to had kept him up hours contemplating life. And he realized that Christianity wasn't the way his parents had taught him while he was growing up. Not at all. There was so much more to it. And Annie was the perfect example of a Christian. Though she didn't know it, she'd even influenced Sean. He'd said if her attitudes were what Christianity was about, he just might be interested.

He'd realized his feelings ran way too deep for this woman and he couldn't commit to her. He couldn't because every time he looked at her he would be reminded of his broken relationship with Christ. If that wasn't proof that he was no good with relationships, he didn't know what was.

When he'd seen Sean kiss her, however, his mind had short-circuited. For one moment, as he'd held her in the limo, he'd thought of spilling his guts and telling her how he really felt, but reality had come crashing back in on him when he'd thought *long-term.* He'd allowed his fear of failed relationships to rule him and sent her away.

He would never forget the devastated look on her face.

As he'd sat there contemplating it, he'd gotten a call from Sean chewing him out for leaving Annie alone on the plane and forcing him to go back to Holland and then a second call saying his son was there and in a panic.

He'd talked to Sean two more times during the night. What he'd told him had stunned him. Annie had actually held his son while he cried and talked to him, comforting him. He was surprised Annie was still there actually.

And then she'd fixed them hot cocoa.

Jealousy reared its head, but Sean scolded him in three languages, telling him what an idiot he was not to accept that Annie loved him and that he loved Annie.

As usual, his friend was right.

Though he wasn't happy with the way Sean had taught him the lesson, he knew Sean was right.

Now, at the house, he saw Sean come walking out in the early dawn light, hands in his pockets, looking pretty weary himself.

"I'm glad you're here. Annie's leaving."

Victor paused. "When?"

"In about twenty minutes. I've put her off as long as I can, but she's got a plane to catch."

He blinked as it dawned on him what Sean meant. "She's going back to America."

Sean nodded.

Victor hesitated. "Because of our fight?"

He shook his head. "No. She says her kids need her. Her daughter is pregnant and wants an abortion and evidently…get ready for this, Jake. We made international TV news, fighting out in front of the club, and Annie was right in the middle of it. Her kids saw the show.

"She's beside herself. Totally humiliated. Said

at one point her reputation was ruined, and she'd probably never be accepted in Brownsville, Louisiana, again.''

He groaned. ''I don't have time for this. I've been on the phone with my lawyer about getting full custody rights to my son. After what I told him, he didn't think it'd be that hard since Josh is thirteen. I need to see to Josh—''

''Josh is asleep. You'd better talk to Annie first.''

Victor nodded and started past Sean.

Sean caught his arm. ''Victor…?''

Victor paused. He finally met Sean's gaze. ''It's okay.'' He shrugged. ''It was only something I've seen you do with a thousand other women on a dozen different sets.''

''Hey,'' Sean said, good-naturedly.

''Okay, maybe not that many leading ladies in the movies, but…I realize now you were trying to get my attention.''

''Did it work?''

Victor paused and nodded. ''Just don't ever do that to Annie again.''

Sean lifted his hands. ''I think of her as a sister,'' he said and smiled.

''You're one sick man,'' Victor replied.

Sean chuckled. ''Okay, I think of her as a sister-in-law, brother,'' he added.

Victor paused, then reached up and clapped Sean on the shoulder.

He continued up the steps. "Where is she?"

"In the library."

He nodded.

Going into the house he paused to glance around. A fishing pole and skateboard propped by the door were the only evidence that his son had arrived.

The floral suitcase by the door was the evidence that Annie was leaving.

He strolled across the room to the library door and tapped, then he entered.

Annie sat in a wingback chair, a book opened in her lap.

It was his poetry.

She quickly closed it and set it aside.

She stood. "Victor," she said and clasped her hands. Her gaze skittered away.

What could he say? "I'm sorry, Annie."

Her gaze touched his and then fled. "It's okay."

He slowly strode across the room and dropped onto the sofa. "I hear you're leaving."

She nodded.

"Your daughter, Sean said. A crisis."

Her shoulders slumped with relief. "Is he still in one piece?" she asked warily.

He nodded. "I was afraid *you* might have taken

him apart after what Sean told me on the phone. Seems he met you at the airport…'' He trailed off to let her elaborate.

She didn't.

Finally, she took a breath. ''Victor, I'm sorry. I'm sorry I led you on. I've had a wonderful time here, but I have got to go home to my kids. They need me.''

Victor blanched at her words. ''Annie, you didn't lead me on.''

She shook her head.

He added, ''And while your daughter might need you, she *is* thirty-two. She's old enough to make her own decisions.''

He thought he found all of this with the kids awfully convenient. So, he thought he had to suggest a possibility. ''Sean told me they saw us on TV. Are you sure that's not why she called and is causing such a ruckus? They've controlled your life for a long time.''

Annie flushed. ''That's not true! Yes, they were upset about seeing me, but Susan is having a real crisis and needs me.''

''They have to start living on their own sometime,'' Victor suggested gently. ''My wife was a lot like the way you've described your kids. She was totally self-serving, wanting only what she wanted. She would do anything to manipulate me into getting it. That's how Josh came about.''

He paused and shifted forward in his chair. Perhaps he shouldn't be taking such a direct approach, but time was short and he thought being blunt was best. ''She told me she was on the pill but she lied because she wanted a child. She was never on the pill, she told me later.''

He remembered the anger and bitterness he'd felt toward her, but how he'd finally let go of that. ''I accepted it because Josh had been born and I loved him. But it was no loss when she left. She's always throwing things away when they become no use to her, just like she's doing with Josh now.''

He thought of his son upstairs and then forced his mind back to the situation at hand.

''I'd like you to stay and let us talk this out. But I'm afraid this problem may take a while to resolve.''

''I can't just leave my kids hanging back in Brownsville,'' Annie said quietly.

''They're grown,'' he countered, wanting to make her get this point so he could then discuss the fiasco of the previous night.

''But they need me.''

Victor sighed. ''You can't let others run your life, Annie. That's what you've been doing your entire life. For the first time in your life, since you've been here, you've been free and doing things that you wanted to do. The painting, the horses, the premiere. You've been living again.''

''Their mom has always told them I'm trash.''

He nodded. Her words only proved what he'd been saying. He hated that she'd received the same knowledge about her stepchildren from him. ''You are anything but, Annie.'' He leaned forward and took her hands. ''Don't let them treat you like trash, Annie.''

She shook her head. ''I'm not. But I can't stay here anyway, Victor.''

''Why not?'' he asked, calmly.

She glanced away and gently pulled her hands from his before clasping them in her lap. ''For the very reasons you gave. I can't let someone else run my life.'' She hesitated, the pain on her face clearly showing in the new lines that formed as she tried to articulate what she wanted to say. Finally, she whispered, ''I love you, Victor, but you have a lot of issues you have to settle in your life. And as long as I'm around, you're going to use me as a substitute for those problems.''

Her words hit him between the eyes.

She loved him.

He'd known it. As much as he had fought it, from the first day he'd seen her, he'd known he couldn't stay away, and he'd known this was exactly what would happen.

He didn't want this.

He wasn't the type to be tied down, especially when he felt so out of control since meeting her.

"There was a man in the Bible called Jacob," Annie continued, and she was oblivious to what was going on inside him. "He ran from God his entire life. He had relationship problems—with his dad, his brother, with God. God had finally to cripple him to get his attention. But when God did that, He renamed him Israel and a nation was born of him, Jake," she said softly and he caught her use of his name Jake.

It was easy to see what she was getting at.

"I'm not running from God," he argued.

"Oh?" she asked.

She glanced at the clock on the mantel and stood. "I have to go, Victor, but I hope you'll consider what I said."

He couldn't believe she was leaving.

He was a total jerk, totally selfish because he wanted her to stay.

"Annie—" he said and stood.

She hesitated and stared at him. He couldn't do it. She was right. He had issues he was dealing with. He didn't want an ever-after type of relationship; he knew it couldn't work…and if he asked her to stay, that's what she'd want. She was a good girl.

"I'm not running from God," he said, and thought, Where did that come from? Out of everything they'd said, for some reason, that was the one thing which had stuck in his mind.

"Goodbye, Victor."

She turned and walked out of the door.

Victor simply stared.

He heard Sean's voice and then the front door open and close.

Eventually, he heard the car start.

The sound of the moving vehicle drifted to him as it drove off.

When all was quiet he finally realized he'd lost Annie.

Because of his stubborn pride and stupidity, he'd lost Annie.

For the first time in so long that he couldn't remember he dropped to his knees and he cried. And while he was there he asked God to show him again what love was.

Eventually he realized that God had indeed been chasing him. And when Annie had come into his life, God, through her gentle words and spirit, had brought him to a place he needed to be.

His bitterness and anger were gone and his

searching heart could once again seek more than empty promises to fill the hole that was left.

And with seeking, he realized there were several things he had to do. His son, his spiritual life… So many things had to be righted.

He stood and crossed to the phone and called his lawyer, with whom he had an intense but productive conversation.

"So, are you going after her?"

He glanced at Sean who had just entered, and asked as he hung up the phone, "Why are you still hanging around?"

Sean smiled. "Because I want to see you do the right thing."

Victor sighed. Going around the sofa, he dropped into a chair. "Has anyone ever told you that you're meddlesome?"

Sean chuckled. "You. Every chance you get. So, are you going after her?" Sean crossed to the sofa and sank down onto it, his legs sprawling out in front of him. Though Sean looked relaxed, Jake knew that inside, his feelings didn't mirror his posture. He could see the dark concern that flickered to the forefront in Sean's eyes when he didn't think Jake would notice.

Victor chuckled. "You don't give up, do you?"

Sean only smiled that smile of his that didn't fool Jake for a moment.

Victor decided to tell Sean the truth. "I'm going to wait for my lawyer to call. He's pretty sure he can get my ex-wife to sign full custody over. Then I'm going to tell my son the good news and in the meantime, I am going to go to church."

"Church? But it's only Thursday." Sean looked at his watch, confirming the date. Casting a quizzical gaze at Victor he said, "You do remember Annie? Who just left you?"

Jake nodded. "But there are things in my life. I need to start over. I have to get my life in order first. Then I can go after her. The small church Annie took us to meets on Sundays, Tuesdays and Thursdays."

"And you're going to go today?"

"Tonight actually. I'm going to take Josh to dinner after I tell him the plans. Then I'm going. Why don't you join us?"

Sean hesitated. "I don't know." It was obvious he didn't understand why Victor wasn't going after Annie immediately. But Victor understood and Victor knew Annie would as well.

"You can work on me some more about going after Annie."

Sean grinned, his attention diverted to what Victor had said. "I don't trick that easily. You won't let me talk during the service."

"We can talk on the way there and back."

"Will you let me lay out the reasons you should go?"

Victor nodded. "And then I'll tell you my reasons for waiting."

"Put that way…" He nodded. "You've got a deal."

Chapter Sixteen

Annie opened the door and was not surprised to find a flower delivery truck in her driveway.

"Mrs. Hooper?"

Annie nodded.

"These are for you."

"Thank you." She took the yellow tulips. They were beautiful.

And they were so appreciated.

Lifting the card, she found it said, *Hoe is het met jou?*

Her fingers trembled as she read the words. There was no name, just that phrase written upon it. Though it sounded familiar, she couldn't remember the translation.

Tulips.

He'd remembered her secret love of tulips.

Never in her life had anyone ever sent her tulips.

She'd arrived home three weeks ago, to the hot humid and very overpowering Louisiana heat. Wilting, she'd come home only to have her daughter stop by and blithely inform her, as she asked for more money, that she wasn't really pregnant. Her daughter had only said that to make Annie realize that it *could* have happened, since Annie wasn't being responsible and was running all over Europe with some movie star.

Annie had been furious. At her daughter and herself. Victor had been right. He'd known without even talking to her daughter that she had been lying.

They'd had a huge argument that had ended when Annie had told her daughter she was cutting the apron strings. Her daughter had thrown a statue, shattering it and Annie had told her to leave until she could treat her better.

It hadn't taken long for her stepson, Mark, to hear of the fight.

He'd shown up, laundry in tow, to test the waters.

Annie had informed him she wasn't a washeteria. And then she'd dropped the bombshell. The money in the trust that their father had left them had been split up. She'd opened accounts for both children and had given them all but enough money to last her for two months.

Mark had been stunned. And then he'd told Annie he loved her and if she needed the money—

But Annie had simply said no. She was glad to know that Mark loved her. She had really begun to wonder. But giving them the money had been for the best. The children had been obsessed with the money their father had left her. By getting rid of it, giving it all to the kids, they would then have no more fuel from their mom against her. They could love her or not. They wouldn't be coming to her begging for money anymore—at least not their daddy's money. Nor hers since she wouldn't have any. She really was starting all over again.

But Victor had changed something in her. She was living again, felt alive and young, despite the fight they'd had. He had changed her in so many ways.

And though she missed Victor dreadfully, she admitted she needed the time away to break free and start her own life.

Which included the new job. Without Harry's money, she would need that job—desperately. She felt more qualified since the art lessons Victor had given her.

She wondered what Victor was up to....

She looked again at the flowers and then, on

impulse, went to the small rolltop desk and pulled out some writing paper. Sitting down, she began to write:

Sitting here alone, in the quiet of the house, I ponder
What is the weather like in Holland and yonder.
Is it still cool and lush and green?
Are the tulips still on the scene?

"It's a letter from Annie," Victor said, wiping his face and sitting down in his chair at work.

He and Sean were doing some extra scenes on the movie that was due out at the end of the year and he'd had his mail forwarded.

"Oh?" Sean asked. He straightened his chain mail and threw the long black strands from the wig back over his neck. "What does she have to say?" Grabbing up a bottle of water he took a long cool swallow.

Victor was already reading.

But none matters without you there,
for what is beauty with an empty soul?
What are flowers and life and cares,
When my heart is now an empty hole?

"She really doesn't write verse well," he murmured, a grin on his face. "But I'll never trade this letter for anything."

"She wrote you poetry?" Sean asked. "Let me see."

Victor held the letter up out of reach.

"I think it's time I finally go visit," he said quietly.

"Finally? It's been nearly two months and you think it's *finally* time you go?" Sean dropped back in his seat with a big grin on his face.

"We're ready for you," one of the assistants said.

Sean stood. "We'll be finished up by the end of the week."

Victor nodded. "I'll be on the plane the next day. Can you watch Josh?"

"What are uncles for?" Sean said.

Victor stood. "Thanks. For everything."

"Anytime," Sean agreed.

"Just remember," Victor said warily. "You promised. No more kissing Annie."

Sean chuckled. He held up his hands. "Now what about at the wedding?"

The growl Victor let out scared the assistant away and had people within the area wondering just what had happened to set those two at it again.

*　*　*

Annie had counted twenty-two bouquets of tulips in her house this morning. She really needed to have a talk with Victor.

She'd found an English-Dutch dictionary and discovered what each message meant. The first one had said simply, How are you. A very apt question after the way she'd been when she'd left. The following day, red tulips had arrived with a note saying, I'm sorry.

Then a bouquet with a note that said, Forgive me.

Followed by notes such as: I'm a fool. You're my life. I got your letter. Be the keeper of my heart. There were more impersonal ones like: God has changed me, along with, my son likes you. He wants to see you again and so do I and I have full custody. She could go on and on. But today the note had translated as: I'll be seeing you.

She smiled at all of the flowers. Though she wasn't in Holland, she felt as if she was living among the tulips. It was breathtaking. And his notes…

She'd even gotten a four-page letter from him last week. It'd been seven weeks since she'd left. She'd started her job early at the Community Center. Her children, though they didn't agree with her living her own life, had made peace and were actually starting to come by more often again.

She was so glad she'd done the right thing with them. She'd written Victor telling him what had happened, but hadn't heard back until the long letter.

She was ecstatic to hear he was in church and had such a hunger for God. He told her how many things he was discovering and that his son had hooked up with the youth group at the church. They had made a big difference in his life and he thought his son was going to heal.

He was worried because he was going to have to do some extra shooting for a movie that was due out in December and his son was going to be home alone with the servants. He said he might even take his son to the set instead.

It had been a wonderful letter.

She missed him so much.

Now in class, waiting for it to start, Annie took some time this morning to work on her own painting. Since she was in the Community Center, she didn't look up when the door opened, she simply said, "Come on in. I'll be right with you."

She was working on a project for her house called Peace. For the first time in years she thought she'd finally come to grips with that. She hadn't realized how little complete peace she'd had until she'd confronted her children.

"Delivery for Mrs. Hooper."

Annie gasped.

She knew that voice.

She darted a glance around the canvas and stared.

Victor Rivers stood in the room smiling and looking so very good to her eyes. His hair was groomed perfectly, having grown back out, she noted, and he had a bit of stubble, probably from the shoot he'd had to do. The shirt and pants he wore complemented his gorgeous masculinity. "You've lost weight."

He smiled.

Then she saw what he had in his hand. "My shoe?"

It was the shoe she'd worn over her cast. "I'm looking for the woman who can wear this shoe. She ran out of my house one morning and I haven't seen her since."

She bit her lower lip, grinning. She slowly shook her head. "I'm afraid it doesn't fit me." She held out her leg to show the cast was gone.

"I'm glad to hear that," he replied and then from behind his back, he brought out the other shoe. "But perhaps this one does?"

Her eyes widened.

He walked forward and knelt down in front of her. "What are you doing, Victor?" she asked.

She saw that every single person from the center was gathered at the door, peeking in. She blushed. Of course, Victor would draw a crowd wherever he went. Oh dear, there was Amy with a video camera.

When he touched her shoe, she looked down. He slipped the loafer from her foot. "Let's try this," he said.

"Victor," she whispered.

She hadn't seen him in forever, but it was like only yesterday. Her heart was hammering, blood racing through her vessels and she even felt lightheaded.

He eased her toes into the shoe and released her foot.

She tried to slip her foot in but something was blocking it.

"Don't tell me this one doesn't fit either?"

She knew that was her shoe and it should fit. She lifted her foot and grabbed the shoe to see what was the matter. "Well it might help if you took this silly little box out..."

She trailed off as she realized just what the box was.

She glanced down at Victor, who was still on one knee before her, and then back at the box. "Open it, Annie," he said.

With trembling fingers, she pried open the lid.

"Will you marry me?"

Her hand went to her mouth. "Oh heavens," she whispered. Inside was a beautifully cut oval diamond.

"I love you, Annie Hooper. I thought my life was great until you came along. But with your crash into my life I was never able to go back to how I was before—on autopilot, simply navigating through life without purpose. Because of you I've found life in Jesus and because of you I've found love again.

"Though these last seven weeks have been some of the best of my life as I've rediscovered my relationship with Christ, they have also been the loneliest of my life. Marry me," he repeated. "I know now that I can do ever after."

Ever after. He'd come to grips with his relationship problems just as she had come to grips with her own weaknesses.

And he wanted her to marry him.

She nodded, unable to say anything.

He took the box and slipped the ring on her finger.

"Now about our wedding," he said as he stood. "We have to have a big wedding. And Sean has already agreed to be my best man. But there's this custom that the best man can kiss the bride. When he tries that I want you to say *ga weg*. Okay?''

Annie tossed back her head and laughed. And then she threw her arms around his neck and kissed him, in front of the gathering students and staff.

He lifted her into his arms, holding her close. Spinning her around in the middle of the room he said, his mouth only a mere breath from hers, ''I'm never going to let you go again.''

''Nor I you, my love. Nor I you. For now and evermore.''

*   *   *   *   *

Dear Reader,

Sometimes ideas just come to you—in the middle of the night. And as any writer will tell you, when that happens you must get up right then and start writing, or else.

This was one of these books.

This has been one of the hardest years of my life, yet God has blessed me richly in my career and my spiritual walk. As I thought of the many areas in which God has blessed me, I thought of the verse in Revelations that tells us we often think we are rich when in reality we're naked.

That's the case for our hero, who has everything money can buy, yet is empty inside because he's missing the greatest gift of all—Jesus Christ.

Enjoy the read, and any mistakes in Dutch are my fault.

Cheryl Wolverton

Love Inspired

ALMOST HEAVEN

BY

JILLIAN HART

She wanted to make a new start—alone. But
Kendra McKaslin couldn't turn Cameron Durango away
from her run-down riding stable. Seeing the handsome
sheriff unlocked painful memories of the past that were
intertwined with his gentle kindness on that terrible
night. Yet perhaps Cameron's appearance was a sign that
all her of dreams were finally coming true….

Don't miss

ALMOST HEAVEN

on sale July 2004

Available at your favorite retail outlet.

THE HEART'S VOICE

BY

ARLENE JAMES

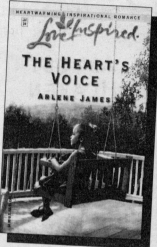

Supporting her two young children and caring for a
dilapidated house, widow Becca Kinder needed the help
of a man—specifically, carpenter Dan Holden, who'd
returned home after time in the service. The ex-military
man was reluctant to get involved with anyone after an
accident that left him unable to hear. But Dan would
soon learn that he had to listen to God's plan—to help
Becca rebuild her home…and her heart.

Don't miss

THE HEART'S VOICE

on sale July 2004

Available at your favorite retail outlet.

www.SteepleHill.com

LITHV

From #1 CBA bestselling and
Christy Award-winning author

DEE HENDERSON

comes her first classic romance.

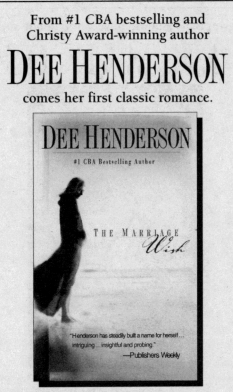

As Scott Williams's thirty-eighth birthday dawned, he was at the top of his game. Or was he? Successful, blessed with friends and a rich faith, his life seemed perfect to others. But something was missing—a family of his own to love.

After making a birthday wish to meet the woman of his dreams, Scott encountered enchanting author Jennifer St. James strolling along the beach. But beneath her beauty lay a heart mourning her late husband and a faith once deep, now fragile. Could Scott's hopes and prayers bring fulfillment for both of their dreams?

Steeple Hill®

**"Henderson has steadily built a name for herself...
intriguing...insightful and probing."
—*Publishers Weekly***

Available in September 2004.

www.SteepleHill.com

SDH519

A gripping suspense novel from debut author

J.F. MARGOS

J.F. MARGOS

Shattered Image

A TONI SULLIVAN MYSTERY

She'd seen it all before, but this time she was left with
nothing to hang on to but her faith.

To forensic sculptor Toni Sullivan, visiting crime scenes is part of her
daily routine and her latest case is nothing out of the ordinary. But
when she accepts a new assignment that may officially prove a
beloved old friend is dead, her emotional cool is shaken to the core.

To find peace, Toni will do whatever it takes to unmask a murderer.
But where will she find the strength to handle the
traumatic legacy of the past? She can only trust that
her prayers for help will be answered.

Steeple
Hill®

Available in September 2004.

www.SteepleHill.com

SJFM520

Love Inspired®

In July look for
Adam's Promise,
the first title in
the dramatic
six-book romantic
suspense series

INSPIRATIONAL ROMANTIC SUSPENSE

Love Inspired

Someone wanted the handsome
doctor out of the way...

Faith
On The Line
BOOK 1

**ADAM'S
PROMISE**

GAIL GAYMER MARTIN

Faith
━━━◆ On The Line ◆━━━

Save $0.75 off the purchase price
of *Adam's Promise*.

**Redeemable at participating retailers in the U.S. only.
May not be combined with other coupons or offers.**

RETAILER: Steeple Hill Books will pay the face value of this coupon plus 8 cents if submitted by the customer for this specified product only. Any other use constitutes fraud. Coupon is nonassignable. Void if taxed, prohibited or restricted by law. Void if copied. Consumer must pay for any government taxes. Valid in the U.S. only. Mail to: Harlequin Enterprises Ltd., Steeple Hill Books, P.O. Box 880478, El Paso, TX 88588-0478, U.S.A. Non-NCH retailers—for reimbursement submit coupons and proof of sales directly to: Steeple Hill Books, Retail Marketing Dept., 225 Duncan Mill Rd., Don Mills (Toronto), Ontario M3B 3K9, Canada. Cash value 1/100 cents. Limit one coupon per customer.

Coupon expires on August 31, 2004.   Manufacturer's coupon

Steeple
Hill®

5 65373 00075 5   (8100) 0 11126

® and TM are trademarks owned and used by the trademark owner and/or its licensee.
© 2003 Harlequin Enterprises Ltd.

Love Inspired

In July look for
Adam's Promise,
the first title in
the dramatic
six-book romantic
suspense series

ADAM'S
PROMISE

GAIL GAYMER MARTIN

Faith
On The Line

Save $0.75 off the purchase price
of *Adam's Promise*.

**Redeemable at participating retailers in Canada only.
May not be combined with other coupons or offers.**

RETAILER: Steeple Hill Books will pay the face value of this coupon plus 10.25 cents if submitted by the customer for this specified product only. Any other use constitutes fraud. Coupon is nonassignable. Void if taxed, prohibited or restricted by law. Void if copied. Consumer must pay for any government taxes. Valid in Canada only. Mail to: Harlequin Enterprises Ltd., Steeple Hill Books, P.O. Box 3000, Saint John, New Brunswick, E2L 4L3, Canada. Non-NCH retailers—for reimbursement submit coupons and proof of sales directly to: Steeple Hill Books, Retail Marketing Dept., 225 Duncan Mill Rd., Don Mills (Toronto), Ontario M3B 3K9, Canada. Limit one coupon per customer.

Coupon expires on August 31, 2004.   Manufacturer's coupon

Steeple
Hill®

52605752

® and TM are trademarks owned and used by the trademark owner and/or its licensee.
© 2003 Harlequin Enterprises Ltd.